Lucy

STRIPES PUBLISHING

An imprint of Magi Publications

1 The Coda Centre,
189 Munster Road,
London SW6 6AW

A paperback original

First published in Great Britain in 2008

Text copyright © Liz Elwes, 2008
Cover photograph copyright © Elisabeth Smith Ltd, 2008

ISBN: 978-1-84715-055-4

The right of Liz Elwes to be identified as the author of this work has been asserted by her in accordance with the Copyright, Designs and Patents Act, 1988.

A CIP catalogue record for this book is available from the British Library.

Printed and bound in Belgium.

To Giles, William, Alice, Thomas and Jamie.
All my family and friends and Zoe
and Ruby Anderson for inspiration.
To Jane Harris and everyone at Stripes for all their hard work.

Lucy

Liz Elwes

Stripes

"Lucy McDonnell! What are you writing? Are you so excited about industrial growth in South America that you felt you had to get started before the rest of the class? Very keen."

I put my pen down and sat very still. I arranged my face into a totally blank expression. In the animal world I would be a mouse and Miss Marshall would be a snake and slide right past me. She would not detect me in my incredible stillness.

Unfortunately, I am a lot bigger than a mouse and incredible stillness cut no ice with a teacher

who had all her senses, including super-power eyesight. She had not only clearly seen me, in spite of being at the back of twenty solid Year 8 pupils, but she had spotted the piece of paper I was trying to edge under my pencil case, too.

She swooped down and snatched it up. "Ah ha! Now let's see what major contribution to learning we have here." I waved my arms after her in pointless protest. If Miss Marshall read that letter out loud I would die of shame. The rest of the class were now all sitting up eagerly watching her. Something interesting had happened in a geography lesson at last.

She sniffed before starting to silently scan the page. I cringed. I knew all too well what it said.

Darling Brad
Last night at the bus stop was brilliant! I really fancy you. If we went out I'd never end it with you. Not even if a really rich footballer fancied me and asked me out as well. I'd say no to him. Even if 'Hello' magazine wanted to

do our wedding and I could have a dress made by a designer for free. I'd still say "No famous footballer, I only want to go out with Brad." Even if I could have a pink glass coach and dyed pink doves. Because you are all I want. When I think of kissing you I...

And that's as far as I'd got. Which was probably just as well. I waited to hear my fate. The worst part of it was that Miss Marshall was now going to think that I had written it. Which of course I had, but how could I explain that it wasn't what it seemed. As if I'd have anything to do with Brad Brown, who is barely one up from the apes. However, Shaynia West loves him with all her heart and she said she'd pay me to write him a love letter. And knowing what she's like, I knew she'd think those words were pure poetry.

Not obviously an opinion shared by Miss Marshall. "Detention tomorrow," she said. "And if

you ever use my class time to write such ridiculous drivel again, I shall send it straight to your parents. Do you understand?"

I nodded dumbly. Maisie gave me a sympathetic wince. Lucas was stuffing his tie in his mouth, trying not to laugh.

"Do you understand?"

"Yes, Miss Marshall."

"That's so unfair!" I wailed, as we walked out of school at the end of the day.

"So what did you write to Brad the Beloved?" Lucas asked, pulling his beanie down on his thick blond hair. "Though come to think of it, could he actually read such a long letter? Maybe you should have simply doodled a few pictures instead, Lucy. A heart, a football boot, a pair of cooing doves and a picture of Brad with the words 'My Hero'... Something romantic like that."

"Shut up..."

"Do you think that's the end of your love-letter business?" Unlike Lucas, Maisie's brown eyes

were brimming with concern. Thank goodness one of my best friends cared about me.

"Well, it's the end of writing them in lessons. If my mum read that letter, I'd die. She's definitely had a sense of humour bypass lately."

"Are you going to tell her about the detention?" Maisie asked.

"I'll have to," I sighed. "The school will send a letter anyway." Detention was bad enough, but I was more bothered about losing the cash. Since Mum and Dad had had to cut my allowance so drastically due to the McDonnell family financial crisis, it had come in very useful.

"Sorry, Lucy." Shaynia wandered over, lugging her bag behind her. She rolled up a stick of gum like a lizard's tongue and pushed it into her mouth. "Any chance you could do me another one?"

"Erm … I'm afraid not. I think I'll have to call a halt for a while."

Her face fell. "That's well miserable of you."

"Detention tomorrow is worse than miserable, Shaynia."

She sighed. "Yeah, s'pose. Well, if you change

your mind, the offer still stands." And she hitched her bag up on to her shoulder and rumbled off to lie in wait for Brad at the gates.

I groaned. "I can't bear the fact that Miss Marshall, and probably the whole staffroom, think that I fantasize about kissing Brad Brown."

Lucas grinned. "Yes, there is a certain irony in the fact that the one girl in the year who isn't remotely interested in any of the boys should end up writing romantic letters to nearly all of them…"

"But they're not from ME!"

He reached forward and ruffled my hair as they climbed on to the bus behind me. "Hey, calm down, Boy. We know." He smiled broadly. "As if!"

I jerked my head away angrily. And I was angry — but not just about the detention. Lucas and Maisie have been my best friends since primary school, and from the first day he met me Lucas had started to call me "Boy". I suppose I had been a pretty wild tomboy then, and I'd never minded. Actually I'd been proud of it. Even in the past few years when I'd got into skateboarding with him and his mates. I'd done gymnastics for years, and my

natural sense of balance and agility made boarding easy for me and I loved it. I was better than any of them now and really enjoyed hanging out at the skatepark and being one of the "boys".

But lately my old nickname had begun to irritate me. And Lucas's recent joking about how I was the only girl in the whole year who didn't fancy anyone was making me feel uncomfortable, too. Even I had noticed that Harry Hopkins in the year above was totally gorgeous, and Deep Patel had a smile that would make any girl go weak at the knees.

I studied my reflection in the bus window. I had to admit I was a bit of a mess. I had always hated getting my hair cut so I'd just stopped a few years ago and taken to scraping it back in a rubber band. Now it was long I wasn't sure what to do with it. Mum used to trim it every now and then, but that's about it. Once in a while she tried to encourage me to have a new style but I always chickened out. It's dark brown and straight. I suppose, if I was totally honest, I'd like to see what it'd look like after a trip to a proper hairdresser.

Maisie told me about a brand-new salon that's

11

opened in town – it's all black and white and ultra cool. Everybody in our class wants to go, but with the money situation as it is there's no chance of me going at the moment.

We had a girly trip into town last weekend and everyone was trying on make-up. I longed to try some, too, so I was glad when Maisie pulled me over and said, "Come on, Lucy, this colour would look fantastic on you. Try it."

Teagan and Georgia were there and burst out laughing. "Lucy! In make-up? She wouldn't know what to do with it!" I felt my cheeks burn with embarrassment. I know they didn't intend to be mean – that's what everyone thinks – but I wished things could be different.

I also wanted to dress in something other than jeans and hoodies. Maisie had offered to come over and have a make-up and shopping session in the holidays, but now she was going to her gran's as soon as term ended so it'd have to wait.

It's difficult to know where to begin on your own, especially if you've always laughed at all that girly stuff. What do you do when you realize you want

to be part of it after all? Maisie says I shouldn't care about what anyone else thinks, but when you've been the class tomboy for ever it's not that easy. She can come into school with a new hairstyle and everyone thinks it's cool.

What would Lucas say if I stopped being "Boy" and turned up with a totally girly haircut? I just know he'd think it was funny. And I didn't want to be laughed at. I don't usually worry too much about what other people think but suddenly, in spite of Maisie's support, I'd gone all self-conscious. It was weird.

Maisie dug her elbow in my ribs, jerking me out of my thoughts. "Hey, Lucy, you're going to miss your stop!"

I jumped up and grabbed my things, waving goodbye as I stumbled out. "See you tomorrow!"

I reached home just before my sister. I opened our front door and let it slam behind me. In her face. She would have done the same to me if she'd got there first. Just because you're sisters doesn't mean you have to get on. Especially if your big sister is as unpleasant as mine. I don't call her

"Millie the Mean" for nothing.

"Hello!"

Mum's voice drifted out from the kitchen. Strange. These days she's never home when we get back from school. I found her sitting at the table nursing a cup of coffee.

"Hi, Mum. What's up?" She couldn't have heard about the detention already – the postal service isn't that good. I dragged my backpack off my back and dumped it on the table. The front door slammed again.

"You are such a stupid freak, Lucy..." Millie stopped at the kitchen door. "Hello, Mum, how come you're back so early?"

"I've got some exciting news for you both." I saw her eyes flick from Millie to me. We couldn't look more different. I mean OK, we had the same brown hair and blue eyes, but my flat school shoes were falling apart, my tights had several holes in them, Millie's hand-me-down school uniform was definitely on the short side, and escaped strands of inadequately-brushed hair fell over my face.

My seventeen-year-old sister, however, looked

perfect. Her long hair was sleek after hours of blow-drying, her pretty oval face was fully made-up; even her spotless white shirt and black trousers looked like they were by some designer. As girly-girls go, Millie was the girliest.

"Come and sit down." Mum patted the chair next to her.

"You're never home early these days. What's all this about?" Millie asked, sliding her bag across the table and pushing mine on to the floor. I ignored it and left it there. It was an argument I'd save for later.

"Yes. What's up, Mum?"

Mum took another sip of her coffee. "Well now girls … I've got some very interesting news I need to tell you both…"

I caught Millie's eye. Then we both quickly looked
away. We're not the kind of sisters who catch each
other's eyes.

"What's all this about?" Millie asked again.

"It's about this," said Mum, and she waved a
large envelope in front of her. "I've been keeping it
a secret, but now it's all confirmed."

I found myself looking at Millie again. She
shrugged her shoulders in a "search me" way.

"It's from your Aunt Jo. We've been emailing
about your grandmother's 70th birthday. She's

having a party this summer, at her house in Calgary. Do you remember it?"

It was seven years since we had been to Canada to visit Gran, but I had vague recollections of a large, colonial-style house with a huge staircase in the hallway and shiny wooden floors.

Mum beamed at us. "She wants us all to go."

"But Calgary's halfway across the world!" Millie protested. "And the end of term is only a week away. All of us? Is Dad invited, too?"

It was no secret that our Canadian grandmother, Mum's mum, did not think a lot of Dad. And as a result he wasn't too fond of her. We all knew she was pretty loaded, but Dad would never accept any help from her. Gran thinks Mum should have married this boring man in Canada called Howard. But Mum ran off with Dad instead, which I could understand as my dad is seriously clever – he was always making things with us when we were young, and now he's built up this building firm based on green principles, which I think is pretty cool.

"No, not Dad," Mum said. "I'm afraid he needs to stay here and try and sort out this contract."

"He'll be devastated," Millie said sarcastically. "But we can't go either, can we? You said we couldn't even afford a weekend by the seaside. So there's no way we can fly halfway across the world for a party."

"Yes," I added, "and I wouldn't want to go anyway."

I was lying though – who wouldn't want to go to Canada? Especially when the alternative was staying at home, doing nothing but hang around the skatepark all summer. But I didn't want Mum to think that I'd be disappointed if we couldn't go. "If I remember rightly," I went on, "Gran was scary and Aunt Jo was some loony hippy and made me eat cattle food – so don't worry, Mum, we don't mind staying here."

Mum raised her eyebrows. "She didn't make you eat cattle food, Lucy! She's just very into, er ... healthy eating. Anyway, you were only six when we were last there so you can hardly remember."

"I *so* can! I chewed and chewed on that grass and lentil stew, or whatever it was she fed us – it looked like a plate of sick."

"I'd be surprised if they let you back in the country anyway, after last time," Millie chipped in.

I gave her a withering glance. "Oh, ha ha ha."

"Well, we all remember you attacking that poor boy. It's a good job you were only six, otherwise you'd have been arrested."

"Shut up."

"No, you shut up."

"Will you both be quiet!" cried Mum. We stared at her. Mum hates rowing. Which is a shame because Millie and I do a lot of it.

Millie looked at her watch. "Look, Mum, Finn's coming round in a minute. It's lovely that Gran's thinking of us and all that; tell her we hope she has a lovely time." She got up from the table and picked up her bag. Mum's arm shot out and pulled her back.

"I haven't finished yet."

Millie grudgingly perched on the edge of her chair, flicking a speck of dust off her trousers.

Mum waved the envelope in her hand. "Your grandmother is so very keen to see us all again that she's sent us our tickets and expenses for the

trip … she wants you girls to see Canada. She says it's part of your heritage."

Mum beamed at us both.

"No thanks." Millie tipped her chair back and put her hands behind her head. "What's the internet for? Tell her thanks again and I'll be sure to look up Canada when I'm next online. I'm confident I'll find it all suitably majestic and moving."

Mum gave her a sidelong glance and continued, "Too late, it's all arranged. Aunt Jo is going to hire a motorhome for us, and the idea is that we pick it up in Vancouver and drive through the Rocky Mountains to Calgary, stopping at places along the way, including their house. It's a beautiful country – you should get to know it better."

"Mum, I'd rather run naked through the school hall than share a confined space with Lucy for even one day. I'd rather share with a moose."

"Millie! Don't be ridiculous."

"What's ridiculous about that? A moose would have a more interesting personality, and it'd definitely smell better."

"I do NOT smell."

"Whatever. It's irrelevant anyway. I'm not going."

I put my head on one side and opened my eyes wide. "Aaah. Will you miss the Stick Insect?"

"Don't call Finn that. Just because no boy would ever look twice at you!"

Millie's boyfriend was finishing school this year and going off to music college. He played lead guitar in a band and was generally considered seriously cool. Finn's great passion, apart from lead guitar, was the piano. Millie played the violin; she passed Grade Seven this term. They met in the music department and the rest is history…

I really like Finn, but Millie's last remark hurt so I carried on. "Will you miss his skinny long legs?"

"ENOUGH!" Mum banged her hand on the table. "Motorhomes – or RVs as they're called – are spacious and comfortable these days with everything you could possibly want: TV, hot showers, loads of space. You'll be fine…"

But Millie wasn't listening. "Why do I have to go? If Dad's not going I can stay with him. Please, Mum, don't make me go. I'll be fine here, and you can go with Lucy and she can wrestle bears and

ride the moose all summer, or whatever you do in Canada. You'll have a great time…"

"Listen to me, Millie. The point is, it's an amazing opportunity for you girls. One that we couldn't normally afford. And anyway, I've already told Gran and Aunt Jo that we're coming. No arguments."

"I'M NOT GOING!" Millie shouted. She got up and walked out, slamming the door behind her.

Mum rested her face in her hands and gave a deep sigh. I reached out and patted her shoulder. "Don't worry, Mum. It'll be all right when we get there, you'll see, we'll all have a great time … I'm looking forward to it already. In fact, I can't wait."

She turned to me and smiled. "Well whatever happens, it'll certainly be an experience…"

3

"Please tell me you're not wearing that?"

I looked down at my top. "What's wrong with it?"

Millie rolled her eyes and banged her huge suitcase shut. "If you don't know, there's no point in me telling you – but don't sit next to me on the plane. I don't want people to think we're related."

I looked down again. I was wearing my used-to-be-favourite pale-blue hoodie. It was faded now and had lost its shape a long time ago, but I was still fond of it. I knew my clothes were all a bit old, and I'd grown out of half of them, but I could hardly

ask Mum for some new stuff at the moment. Even Millie had stopped asking.

It was the morning of our flight to Canada and to say the atmosphere was strained would be an understatement. Millie was raging about leaving Finn.

"His band is touring and I won't even be in the same country!" she had wailed to Mum. Finn's tall figure had just walked sadly down our front path. His black, skinny jeans and dyed black hair reflected the general mood.

The week had gone so fast since Mum had told us we were going. I'd met up with Maisie and Lucas over the weekend and they had both been so pleased about my news.

Maisie had lent me a couple of T-shirts. "I don't expect I'll be out of my jumpers the whole holiday," she sighed. "The weather forecast for Scotland is horrible. Lucky you, going to Canada."

"Look out, Canada! Here comes Boy!" Lucas had said. "We'll miss you at the skatepark, but I want to hear all about how you fought bears and stuff when you get back."

24

"And I want to hear all about those gorgeous Canadian boys." Maisie had put her hand to her forehead in a fake swoon. "I'm so jealous I can hardly bear it."

There had been loads to do, which was a good thing as Mum hadn't had time to dwell on the detention letter.

"Tell me again what you were writing to Brad in class?" she had asked frowning, but she had been too distracted by her increasingly long "to do" list to concentrate very much on my mumbled answer.

But this morning I could see she was not only busy, but stressed. I guessed it was about leaving Dad with too much to do on his own.

"Don't worry, Mum," I said, giving her a hug. I decided to change the subject and ask for a Canadian family update.

"So, what does Aunt Jo do now?"

Mum looked grateful for the distraction. "Well, she's set up a company selling hand-knitted sweaters in the mountain resort where they live. She designs them herself and they've got big moose and bears on the front, that kind of thing."

Now even me, with my limited dress sense, could tell that that could not be a good look.

"I think it's going pretty well," Mum continued, "and your Uncle Hector owns a big insurance business."

"Does that mean they're rich?" I asked.

"Lucy!" Mum frowned disapprovingly. "Let's just say they're comfortable."

"Does Gran like Uncle Hector better than Dad?"

Mum paused for a moment before answering. "Your grandmother always thought that Hector would be a good, solid husband for your Aunt Jo, and actually she was right."

"What about Mexico and Cuba?" I gave Mum a look. She grinned.

"I know your cousins have unusual names, but that's Jo for you. Mex, goodness, he must be sixteen now and Cuba, she's a year older than you, so she's fourteen. I don't expect I'll even recognize them. I do remember Mex never said a word."

"Never?"

Mum shook her head. "Hardly ever. Just the occasional grunt."

"So it's a good thing that we'll only be staying with them for one night on the way, and that's all we'll see of them until Gran's party."

"Lucy!"

"Well, it's true. I just wish we only had to spend one day with your friend Sarah, too."

"Tough!" said Mum. "She's my best friend from high school and I want to spend time with her. Imagine if you and Maisie lived thousands of miles apart? Wouldn't you want to see as much of her as you could if you had the chance?"

"You email all the time."

"That's not the same."

"But *Kane* will be there."

"You haven't seen Kane for seven years, Lucy. People change; you can't judge everyone on what they were like when they were little."

"He was a bully. He scarred me for life!"

"Lucy, he'll be fourteen now, not seven, so I doubt you'll be in any danger. And if I remember rightly, it was six of one and half a dozen of the other with you two. Anyway, it's only for a couple of nights."

"I'd better take some body armour then…" I muttered, lugging my suitcase down the stairs.

"Don't be such a drama queen," Millie sneered, coming down the stairs behind me. "He's hardly going to punch you in the mouth again, but quite honestly, I wouldn't blame him if he—"

"Stop that, Millie," Mum snapped. "Lucy bit his hand in retaliation, if you remember. Sarah and I made them 'make up' and the whole incident was forgotten."

"No it wasn't," I growled.

Mum ignored this comment and swept on, "And you adored his big brother, Bodey, didn't you? You followed him around the whole time … and he's going to be there."

I felt my face turning pink, so I busied myself with the straps on my suitcase. I knew it was crazy – I hadn't seen him for years – but I was feeling excited about seeing Bodey again. I mean, who wouldn't want to meet a sixteen-year-old cool Canadian boy? And I suppose it wouldn't be hard to ignore Kane. I wished I'd had the chance to talk to Maisie about all this, but she had dashed off to

Scotland the day term ended, having made me promise faithfully to bring back a photo of a bear. Lucas had been around but I was hardly going to discuss that kind of thing with him.

Dad came up and hugged Millie and me goodbye. Then he kissed Mum. "Have a great time all of you, you deserve it."

"We'll miss you, Dad," I said. "Good luck with the contract thingy."

Dad smiled. "Thanks." Then he looked at Mum.

She sighed. "You must do what you think is right, David. I know you're incapable of doing anything else, anyway." She grinned and gave him a hug.

Millie banged her suitcase against the front door. "Come on then," she ordered sharply. "Let's go if we're going…"

"So what do you think? Marvellous, isn't it?"

Mum, Millie and I stared, open-mouthed.

It was hard to say which was the most unexpected sight: the dilapidated pink hulk of metal in front of us, or the similarly bulky presence of Aunt Jo standing next to it.

"Surprised, huh? I'll bet." She beamed at us and proudly banged the motorhome on the side as if it were an old shire horse that had just done a hard day at the plough.

"Knew Chuck and Doreen had one down here in

30

Lucy

Vancouver at their daughter's house, had a word and they were only too pleased for us to collect the old girl and for me to drive her back home. So we hired a car, picked her up and here we are! What do you say?"

"Well," Mum croaked, "goodness, it's just all so … so unexpected."

"I know!" Aunt Jo clapped her hands gleefully. "I thought to myself, Jo, Clemmie and her girls are coming over. It's holiday time, so why not join them on the trip? Let the girls get to know their cousins."

For indeed, the pink motorhome and Aunt Jo were not the only surprises. Standing silently at her side were two figures. Cuba and Mex. Cuba was small with round, brown eyes peering out from shoulder-length, light-brown hair. She was on the sturdy side, like her mum. But unlike her mum, she was wearing a startling amount of make-up for a fourteen-year-old.

Mex was thin, in fact, he made Finn look chunky. He was at least six foot, and it looked like his bones were made of cooked spaghetti. He opened

one of his curtains of dark, straight hair just long enough to say a mumbled, "Hi," before disappearing behind it again and going back to gazing at the ground. You'd think children raised on nothing their mother hadn't harvested and cooked herself would look healthier. She gave them a push towards the door.

"Come on, you guys! The kids are dying to show you round!"

I looked at Mum. There was no pretending that this was an RV — not in the sense she had described them. The RVs Mum had described to us stood in gleaming, silver and white palatial splendour, further along in their own special bay in the airport car park. Where all the normal people were heading.

"I didn't know they knitted sweaters that size," Millie muttered, watching the back of Aunt Jo manoeuvring herself with some difficulty through the door. "I swear that bear was actually life-size."

"Shh, Millie," Mum hissed. "That's very rude. Oh for goodness' sake, what are you doing now?"

"Trying to find the map so I can work out exactly

Lucy

how many days, minutes and hours I have to be stuck in Road Trip Hell with Mr Chatty and Little Miss Cheerful. And what's with all that make-up on her anyway?"

"Your aunt believes in letting Cuba express her personality in her own way. Let me see, what did she say on the phone ... she must let Cuba go where her spirit takes her."

"Obviously straight to the cheap make-up counter, then," Millie muttered behind me, as we clambered on board.

"She's called Rambling Rose," Aunt Jo explained, after we had all squeezed in, "because she's pink and she—"

"Yeah, I get it," Millie interrupted. Mum gave her a warning nudge.

"Your mom and I will share the double bed, which is here." Aunt Jo pulled back a white curtain sprigged with pink roses attached to a cord strung across the interior with wooden clothes pegs. I looked at Mum, who is normal size, which means not skinny, and I looked at Aunt Jo. "Cosy" was the word that sprang to mind.

"Then Millie and Lucy will have the single beds – they're those seats on either side of the table during the day. And Cuba will have the bunk above the roof of the driving seats."

Millie and I looked at where we'd be and our eyes narrowed. We hadn't shared a room since we were little kids and those beds looked awfully close.

"Mex has brought a tent, so he'll camp outside – don't want to embarrass you girls!" Aunt Jo chortled. "Obviously there's the gas stove in here and the chemical toilet, which will have to be emptied every time we stop…"

I saw Millie's nose screw up in disgust.

"I'm afraid the shower is a bit of a trickle and the hot water's a bit temperamental, but isn't that exactly what makes it all the more fun? So much better than one of those modern, soulless motorhomes. We'll be like real pioneers! Now let's get you unpacked. You've only seen the car park so far – we need to get you out of here to see the real Canada."

After we had unpacked essentials into all the little

cupboards and nooks and crannies, Millie slumped down on one of the pale-green checked seats, dragged a faded cotton red and white patchwork cover over her head, to indicate her disgust at her surroundings, and began to fume silently.

Aunt Jo raised her eyebrows as she squeezed her way up to the driver's seat at the front.

"Giving off a bit of a hostile vibe, isn't she?" she hissed loudly at Mum as she went past. "Let's hope this trip helps her to nourish her inner spirit."

Mum opened her mouth, then closed it. She was too exhausted by the journey to argue.

"I think I'll have a quick sleep, if you don't mind," she said instead. "It's been rather a long flight."

"Really? I was looking forward to a good catch-up!" Aunt Jo looked sulky, but then she appeared to realize that this wasn't showing the right inner spirit. "Of course, you must rest if you need to. Go ahead, it'll take us a while to reach the ferry to Vancouver Island. I'll wake you when we get there."

Millie went to crash out with Mum on the double bed. I didn't blame her, it looked soft and comfy. The inside of Rambling Rose was old fashioned,

with its painted, white wooden cupboards and counters, but there was something about the clean, faded floral curtains and quilted patchwork covers that I couldn't help finding attractive.

Mex got out his iPod, plugged himself in, and wordlessly went to sit up front with his mum.

This left me and Cuba staring at one another across the table.

I decided I'd at least try to be friendly.

"So what's this Vancouver Island like?" I asked politely.

Cuba stared at me for a second, lowered her head into her arms in front of her on the table, and began to heave with silent sobs.

I cast my eyes wildly around for help. I could see
that Mum was asleep already and if Millie was
awake under her cover she wasn't letting on.
Meanwhile, Aunt Jo was keeping up a running
commentary on every blade of grass that we
passed and had failed to notice that no one was
listening. Mex had his headphones rammed into
his ears and his feet up on the dashboard, his eyes
firmly closed.

I gave a quiet cough and shuffled uncomfortably
in my seat. "Is everything all right, Cuba?" Cuba

raised her head from her arms and gave me a glare of pure hatred. I reared back.

"No," she hissed, "everything is not 'all right'. You've ruined my summer, in fact you've ruined my life!" She placed her head back on her arms again.

"What? Me personally?" I was not the sort of person to let a comment like that go unchallenged.

She flicked her eyes upwards. "Yes! You and your stupid family. If you hadn't had to come to Canada, I wouldn't have to be here on this dumb trip and I could be home in Banff with..." Cuba burst into fresh sobs.

Oh, here we go, I thought. I recognized the signs. *It's all about a boy.*

"Is there a boy you like? In Banff?" I ventured.

"Like!" she screeched. "I don't *like* him. I love him. And if it weren't for you, I'd be spending the whole summer with him." Two fat tears spilled out of her round, brown eyes. I wasn't that moved. I felt an urgent need to defend the McDonnell clan.

"Well, it's not our fault. We didn't know that you were coming on this trip with us. I mean, it's not as if we invited you or anything. If you're really looking

for someone to blame, blame your mum. It was her decision to do this trip all of us together, not ours. You're not the only one missing her boyfriend, you know. And Finn's a lot further away."

I glanced out of the window as a shiny white RV came flying past. A dark-haired boy had his face pressed against the window, and when he saw me, he broke into a grin. I ignored him and turned away.

"Finn!" Cuba snorted. She'd seen his photo when it had dropped out of Millie's bag as we were unpacking. "He's hardly in Don's league. I mean Finn dresses so weird and everything. Your mom must hate your sister hanging out with him. He looks awful."

To be fair, Mum and Dad had done a double take when they first met Finn, but after they had got to know him and it was obvious he was crazy about Millie and serious about his music studies, they'd grown to like him.

"No, they really like him. They tend not to judge people on appearances," I said meaningfully.

"Like I ever would!" she retaliated hotly. "Mom says we can only judge people on their hearts.

Don's got an amazing spirit. He is truly a sharing person. He is captain of the basketball team and so popular. He's simply crazy about me and I'm crazy about him."

Well good for you, I thought, then I frowned — out of the corner of my eye I could see that the boy in the RV was grinning at me again.

"You'll meet him when we get home. Then you'll see who's got the best boyfriend," Cuba declared.

"I'll look forward to meeting him then," I lied. I'd had enough of hearing about the marvellousness of Don. I watched as Grinning Boy's RV pulled into a petrol station in front of us. Good. That's got rid of him. Now I could look out of the window without anything spoiling my view. There was something about the cocky way that he'd looked at me that had been annoying. As if he knew me and knew I thought he was gorgeous.

I must have dozed off because the next thing I knew I was waking up with my face pressed against the glass, and Rambling Rose was wheezing up to the queue for the ferry to Vancouver Island. Mum and Millie had also woken

up and Millie came over to sit with us at the table.

"What on earth is that boy staring at?" Millie asked.

I turned to look. In the line next to us, right alongside, Grinning Boy was back. He gave a wave.

"He's looking at *you*!" Millie shrieked. "The poor deluded boy, and he's not hideous. Maybe I should write him a note and hold it up, 'You're wasting your time – she hates boys.' What do you think?"

"Very funny."

Millie peered around me to get a better look.

"He's still looking – what do you make of that?"

"I think he's incredibly rude."

"Oh! He just waved again." Millie waved back. "Hello! She's here!" Millie mimed, "She 'heart' you," against the glass and pointed at me.

"What are you doing, Millie! Will you *please* just ignore him." I looked around for back-up, but Mum was deep in conversation with Aunt Jo.

"Oh for heaven's sake, Lucy. Where's your sense of humour?"

"Why don't you like boys?" Cuba asked, suddenly.

"I don't ... not like boys," I muttered through gritted teeth.

Millie sighed dramatically. "She's just not interested – a total tomboy. You've never been near having a boyfriend, have you, Lucy?"

"Seriously?" Cuba's pink lipglossed mouth went into an "O" shape of wonder. This fact seemed to have caught her interest enough for her to decide to speak to me again.

"You've never even been out on a date?" she asked.

"Just leave me alone will you!" I snapped.

Millie raised her eyebrows at Cuba and opened her mouth to speak...

"I hope I'm not hearing any aggressive vibes in the atmosphere," Aunt Jo called, as Rambling Rose lurched forward on to the ferry. "Peaceful vibes only on this trip..."

Mum nodded. "Quite. We'll soon be arriving on Vancouver Island. I need some peace and quiet to concentrate on reading the map and getting us to our campsite."

6

"Hiya, Blue-eyes!"

I leaped three feet into the air and the tins balancing on top of the large brown paper bag I was clutching went rolling down the dirt path.

Blocking my way was Grinning Boy.

Mex put down his bag and began to chase the cans. We had been to the local grocery store with a list from Aunt Jo. She was settling Rambling Rose into her "hook up" on the campsite, which meant a parking space with electricity. No sooner had our trusty vehicle shuddered and sighed to a halt than

Aunt Jo had begun writing her "chores" list. For a laid-back hippy she was surprisingly tough when it came to sharing the workload. My first task was to go to the store with Mex. Millie had briefly considered mutiny, but when Aunt Jo handed her the chopping board, she took it without a word.

The boy didn't move. "Surprised to see me?" He raised a cheeky eyebrow. "Isn't that a great coincidence, us staying in the same place?"

The answer to that question was a loud "NO". When we had rolled off the boat I had hoped that I'd never see Grinning Boy again. And now here he was, right in front of me. Standing way too close.

I gathered myself as Mex placed the retrieved cans back in my bag.

"You gave me a fright," I mumbled.

The boy looked pleased. "I can see that. Didn't mean to startle you." He looked at Mex. "Your brother?" Mex gave him a cool look, but said nothing.

"My cousin, and we've got to be going now."

He didn't step out of my way. "I love your English accent, it's so cute. You must be on

Lucy

vacation. How neat is that, us staying at the same RV site? Must be fate or something. Here long?"

I sighed deeply. I could see that lots of girls would think this boy was good-looking. He was tall, with dark, curly hair, blue eyes and a casual, easy smile. I knew Maisie and the other girls in my class would love getting attention from a boy like that, but as far as I was concerned he was full of himself and invading my personal space. I'd never spoken to him before and he was acting as if we were best mates.

"Want to meet up later?"

I took a step back. "No thanks. I'm busy."

"Tomorrow?"

"No. We're going out all day."

He frowned. You could tell he was used to things going more smoothly than this. "OK, well, see you when you get back, then; I'll come by. Name's Craig. Want me to walk you back?"

I looked up at Mex. "No, I'm fine."

"I'll tag along, then."

I groaned inwardly. Mex and I walked in silence through the tall pines back to Rambling Rose, with

Craig informing us all about his successful life in high school in Vancouver and how his family often came here for weekends. I noticed he didn't bother to offer to carry my bag of groceries, though. Or ask what my name was.

When we got back, Millie was ferociously chopping shiny red and yellow peppers on the table outside.

When she saw Craig, she stared in surprise.

"Hello!" she cried merrily. "Didn't know we'd be seeing you again." She raised her eyebrows at me. I gazed up at the pine trees.

"I know," he smiled lazily. "Cool, isn't it?"

And I think he'd have sat down and moved in, if Aunt Jo hadn't appeared at the doorway and said that we were eating in ten minutes and needed to lay the table. He hesitated, she stood there, and he backed off. "See you tomorrow, er…?"

"Lucy," Millie offered. "And this is Mex and I'm Millie."

He winked at me, before disappearing back along the path.

"Lucy's got a boyfriend! Lucy's got a boyfriend!"

46

Millie chanted as she scraped the peppers into a bowl.

"I have not got a boyfriend," I replied hotly. "I don't know him. And I definitely don't like him."

Millie sighed. "Of course you don't like him, Lucy. You don't like any boys. But seriously, you should think hard about this one. He's actually not bad looking and, amazingly, he appears to think that you're worth a second glance."

"Millie! Have you got those vegetables?" Aunt Jo stuck her head out of the window.

"They're right here." Millie stood up and passed them through to her. "Have you seen Cuba? She was supposed to be helping me."

"Cuba is taking a call from Don," Aunt Jo replied.

Before Millie could respond, there was a sizzling hiss as the chopped vegetables hit the butter and garlic in the large pan on the stove. Aunt Jo was insisting that we all went veggie and Mum had promptly insisted on sharing the cooking duties, fearing an onslaught of mung beans and lentils. "I'm simply not letting you do all the work, Jo," she'd said, returning a large bag of bean sprouts to

the fridge. "Let's just keep it simple."

By the time Cuba emerged we were all sitting in front of steaming bowls of pasta with cheese melting on top. If this is how we were going to eat I could do being a temporary veggie quite happily.

"Was that the boy in the RV?" Cuba asked as she sat down. "I saw him through the window."

"Can we talk about something else?" I snapped.

"Yes, that's Lucy's boyfriend," Millie mumbled, through a mouthful of bread and butter.

"Lucy?" Mum looked up enquiringly.

"No he isn't!"

"He's cute!" Cuba piped up. "You could do a lot worse." Her conversation with Don had obviously cheered her up. "He's good-looking. And from what I can gather it's not like you've had that much success with boys so far." She gave a smug smile. "I'd go for it if I were you."

"That's nonsense," Mum interrupted. "Lucy doesn't have to be interested in boys yet. I didn't have my first boyfriend until I was sixteen."

"And I was eighteen!" Aunt Jo added. "Cuba, you must appreciate that not everyone is as keen on

boys as you are. Lucy will get there in her own time."

"Can we please change the subject?" I muttered.

Cuba gave me a sympathetic look. "Of course. Sorry, Lucy. But I could help you with some make-up if you liked. Don't you think I should, Millie?"

Millie nodded. "But it's the clothes as well…"

"Hello? I'm right here," I called out. "And can we talk about something other than me and boys?"

Cuba smiled at me. "So if you're not interested in a good-looking, confident, outgoing boy like him, what kind of boy are you looking for?"

"Kane," laughed Millie.

"Ha ha," I barked.

"You liked Bodey though, didn't you?" she said, her eyes glinting. "Last time we were here you followed him around the whole time."

"I was six years old!" I protested.

"Maybe that's it. Maybe Bodey is the boy you're holding out for!" Millie teased.

"That's enough!" Mum cried. "Lucy asked you to change the subject. There's more to life than boys."

"You are so pathetic," I hissed at Millie as I got up to start the washing-up – number six on my list

of chores. But as I furiously scrubbed a bowl, I found I couldn't stop myself imagining meeting Bodey again. What would he think of me now? I looked down at my too-short jeans and faded hoodie. Probably not a lot.

"He is cute, you know."

Cuba hadn't been able to shirk drying duty and was smearing a cloth around a glass.

"What?" I jumped.

"Craig of course, who else? I know you don't want to talk about it, but you should think very carefully before turning your nose up at him."

"I'm not turning my nose up, Cuba, I just don't think his inner spirit is easy to like. And anyway, some of us manage fine without a boyfriend."

"I couldn't agree more," Mum said, as she brought in some more dishes. "Don't worry about it, Lucy, get out and enjoy life. You'll know when it's the right time for boyfriends."

I hoped she was right. But later, as I lay in bed, I couldn't help wondering if I was the only one who found being a girl so confusing.

7

My bed was surprisingly comfortable, and I don't know if it was that or the fresh air but we all slept so soundly that Aunt Jo had to work hard to get us up for our day out.

But it had been worth missing some sleep for. We had left first thing to drive to the harbour, where we were catching a boat to go whale watching. The sea had been rough, and we'd got soaked by the waves spraying over the side, but it was a small price to pay to see their massive dark shapes slip through the water, so huge and so unconcerned with us

tiny humans. It made me feel part of a much bigger world. Canada was beginning to have that effect on me. It was just so epic; the sky, the scenery, the ocean. Even Millie, who always found something sarcastic to say about everything, was humbled into silence as the whales swam majestically past on their mysterious journey.

After a whole day out on the boat with everyone, I wanted to be on my own for a while, so I walked down through the pines to the sea. Someone had made a fire earlier and I put another piece of driftwood on it.

I would have to go back for supper chores soon, but I needed time to think about things. Sitting watching the waves wash over the rocks under the huge sky made me feel small, and I hoped that would make my worries feel small, too.

I made a list of them in my head:

Worry Number 1: My appearance.

Last night Cuba had nagged me into submission and I'd agreed to a makeover. And I have to admit I was a little bit curious about how I'd look. After an age sitting still while she stabbed and swirled

brushes on my face, she stepped back to admire her handiwork. "Sooo much better, Lucy."

Millie had then walked in. She did a double take. "Lucy. I hope you're aware that two tarantulas have just landed on your face." She peered more closely. "Oh no, my mistake, it's mascara." She turned to Cuba. "She's not going out like that."

"I think she looks great," Cuba replied, defending her handiwork.

"Oh she certainly does," Millie drawled, "for a ventriloquist's dummy." And when I'd looked in the mirror, I had had to agree with Millie on that one. My cheeks were glowing neon pink, nicely matching my gooey lips, and Cuba had chosen an interesting bright-blue eyeshadow. I looked like Coco the Clown's girlfriend. As I set to work with tissues and cleanser I'd had to try really hard not to cry. I felt such an idiot. I had secretly harboured a hope that I would look all grown up and gorgeous. But I looked ridiculous. Just as I'd feared.

Worry Number Two: Boys.

I kept thinking about what Millie and Cuba had said about Craig. Was I mad not to like him?

Maybe I could try a bit harder to change how I felt. But if I did, it might end up with me having to kiss him, and every time I thought about that I felt sick.

Was that normal? Or was everyone right to be so into boys and was I just weird? I wished Maisie was around to give me some advice about what to do. At least she's kissed a boy, even if it was Sam Bailey, also known as Snogger-Sam due to him having snogged half the girls in our year.

Would I ever find a boy I liked? And would I know what to do if I did?

Watching the girls in my class, liking a boy meant flirting and being cool and coyly twirling your hair around your finger. I wouldn't know where to begin without feeling self-conscious and stupid. It was all terrifying.

I sighed. I was destined to die alone in a flat with a hundred cats.

"Hey! Lucy!" I looked up – four figures were approaching across the rocks. My heart sank.

"Look who we bumped into on our way to find you!" Cuba called out.

Hopping from rock to rock next to her and Millie,

was Craig, and a young girl who turned out to be his sister. She was carrying a huge bag of marshmallows.

"You've found my fire!" Craig cried triumphantly, as if he'd invented it or something. I got up to head back, but Cuba, lured by the temptation of forbidden E-numbers and white sugar, fell upon Craig's invitation to join them.

"Mom won't mind if we're a bit late," she gabbled, spearing a pink marshmallow on a stick. Craig sat down next to me and started to throw some driftwood he'd collected on the fire. He pretended to shiver. "Need to huddle up, everyone!" he laughed, moving even closer. Every time I leaned away, he leaned with me. I could see Millie watching. I knew she would be finding it hilarious. And Cuba made an encouraging face, as she stuffed in another marshmallow.

I decided to at least make an effort. I would show them that I could be grown up around boys.

"So, you play American football?"

"Sure do, best in the team. Play baseball, too."

"Best at that, too?" I ventured a guess.

"Sure am."

"Anything you're not best at?" I asked.

Cuba glowered at me.

Craig actually decided to give this flippant remark serious thought before shaking his head. "Nope, can't think of anything."

"How lovely it must be to be you."

Craig nodded. "Yeah, you know, it kinda is…"

"Do you have a girlfriend?" Cuba asked bluntly.

He shook his head and gave me a dazzling smile. "Not at the moment, unusual for me … do you have a boyfriend, Lucy?"

There was a moment of silence and everyone looked at me.

"No, I don't," I said lightly, though I was cringing inside. "I'm fine as I am," I added, more pointedly, hoping Craig might get the hint.

He didn't. He leaned in closer. This was awful. What was I supposed to say now?

I need not have worried – Craig happily filled in the next fifteen minutes talking about himself, while I got a crick in my neck from leaning sideways in an attempt to avoid any physical contact.

Lucy

Just when I'd decided I could stand it no longer and was going to leap up and hurl myself into the sea, Cuba put her toasting stick down, licked her sticky fingers and announced, "Come on, Millie, we're on store duty today, we'd better get going."

I began to get up. Cuba pushed me back down. "No, no! You can stay a bit longer, you went to the store last night." She turned to Craig. "Would your sister like to come along with us?"

Craig's sister leaped up. I glared at Millie but she smiled gaily back and said nothing.

Traitor. They began to walk away up the shoreline.

There was no way I was being left behind with Craig. I began to scramble up.

"Hey, don't you want to stay awhile?" His mouth turned down at the corners.

"No, I mean, erm… I have to go now. I have to help get supper ready, my aunt's very strict…"

He got up to walk alongside me.

"But your cousin said you didn't have to get back yet…"

What did I have to do to get rid of him? Didn't he take a hint?

"I've got to look for something on my way back."

"Why?"

"Part of a school project, biology, we have to find a native plant specimen…"

"What kind of plant are you looking for?"

I started to walk faster to try to catch up with the others, but it was difficult on the rocky beach. I looked around for inspiration.

"Seaweed!" I regretted saying that as soon as it was out of my mouth.

We walked along a bit further.

"So aren't you going to take some?" he asked.

"Take what?"

He pointed at the seaweed-covered rocks. "There's heaps here. How much do you need?"

I took a deep breath. "Only a little."

I bent over and grabbed a large slippery handful from the nearest rock.

He frowned. "How do you know if that kind of seaweed is a native specimen? There's more than one kind on this beach, you know."

My fingers tightened around the slimy, dark-green strips in my hand. Great, Craig was a grade

A biology student, too!

"I just know, OK!" I snapped.

I saw Cuba look back.

And everything would have been all right if he had left it at that and I had caught up with the others, but then he tried to put his arm around me. I wriggled my shoulder to shake it off. Forcing myself to like him was never going to work. Aunt Jo would say, "Listen to your inner spirit." I was, and it was saying, "Yuck!"

He tried to pull me close again. "I really like you."

"That's nice of you to say, Craig," I winced, drawing away, "but I'm just not interested, sorry."

"I'm interested in you," he murmured, moving his head closer to mine.

"But I'm not interested in you…" I said, moving my head as far away as possible.

But Craig took no notice. His eyes had closed in a dreamy way and he was pulling me towards him… And then my natural instinct took over…

A bird flew up, startled, as I walked back through

the pine trees towards Rambling Rose. Millie and Cuba were stomping along beside me.

"What were you thinking?" Millie shrieked.

"I don't know," I mumbled.

"You shoved a handful of seaweed in his face!"

"And you pushed him over," Cuba gasped.

"That was an accident. He lost his balance."

"Really? Honestly, one minute we're all walking home and the next minute we're performing first aid on some boy you've decked."

"I didn't deck him. He fell over."

"Due to the shock of having a handful of green slime unexpectedly slapped in his mouth! What is the matter with you?" Cuba sighed.

I felt exasperated. Craig had run off, dragging his sister behind him, shouting abuse about me being a mad boy-hating freak. I needed to defend myself.

"He tried to kiss me."

"So?" Cuba sighed.

"So I didn't want him to."

"Well I think we can all safely say that he got that message loud and clear. Sometimes a simple 'no' can be just as effective, you know."

"I said 'No!' twice. But he totally ignored me. So my natural survival instinct took over."

I dug my hands in my pockets and kicked a pine cone. It was so unfair! He had deserved it.

Millie suddenly threw back her head and let out a peal of laughter.

"Did you see his face?"

"I don't think it's anything to laugh about," Cuba said. "Lucy is never going to get a boyfriend if she carries on like that."

"You don't get it, do you?" Millie managed to control her giggles. "Lucy doesn't *want* a boyfriend. All I can say is thank heavens we're leaving here tomorrow. Just try and remember to stop and think before you hurl yourself into action next time … especially as we'll be seeing Kane. Is there any possibility that you can refrain from any more grievous bodily harm this holiday?"

8

"Lucy, come and say hello."

Sarah beamed and waved me forward. I had been trying to hover in the background since we had all spilled out of Rambling Rose on to the large tarmac driveway. It had been a long, hot journey. I had had plenty of time to brood over what had happened with Craig and I had come to a conclusion – I was hopeless around boys and I was not going to have anything to do with them for the rest of the trip.

Rambling Rose was hissing with exhaustion after

hauling us up the Rocky Mountains. And they were enormous. The distant peaks still had snow on them, while the lower slopes were covered in huge forests of green pines that rolled off into the distance. Sun Peaks was basically a winter ski-resort, but Mum said it had loads to do for summer visitors, too.

Bodey stepped forward with long, smooth strides. "Yo! Lucy!" He smiled and gave me a friendly hug. I watched him as he welcomed Millie and the others as well. He was exactly as I had imagined. Tall, tanned, with tangled dark-blond hair and light-blue eyes, and totally at ease with himself, the way older boys can be.

I couldn't help breaking into a big smile in response to his warm welcome. Maybe it wasn't the wisest decision to say I'd have nothing to do with boys for the rest of the trip. Maybe what I needed was more practice attracting the right ones.

Sarah looked around. "Where is Kane? I've called him twice. I tell you, ever since we let him have that skateboarding pipe in the back yard we never see him."

"Kane, come over here, now!" she yelled. Right at the end of the garden Kane was skateboarding. We watched him continue for a few moments before he raised his head and began to slowly saunter towards us across the huge lawn.

"At last!" Sarah said as he reached us. "Let's hope Lucy and you get on better this time than on your last visit!" She and Mum doubled up. Why are grown-ups so embarrassing? Did they honestly think that either Kane or I needed reminding? Or thought it was funny?

Kane was tall, nearly as tall as his older brother, and as tanned, but he was stockier and more broad-shouldered, with shoulder-length dark hair. There was no way I would have recognized him from the skinny boy of seven years ago. He flipped his skateboard with his foot and caught it with his hand. In the brief flash of eye contact, I could see that his blue eyes were darker and more intense than Bodey's, and definitely not as smiling. It was no more than I expected. He obviously hadn't changed much. A hug from him would be unthinkable... I nodded curtly. I would not be going to practise

being attractive with him, that was for sure.

"You two, honestly!" Sarah cried. "Well, come on in. Dinner's ready. You must be exhausted after that drive. Gerry's got the barbecue all ready."

Millie nodded a brief hello to Kane, but before he could respond a muffled voice cried out from Rambling Rose, "Wait for me!"

It was Aunt Jo. She had decided the evening mountain air called for one of her sweaters and had gone back to find one. She emerged with a giant moose covering her ample bosom.

"Jo has a knitwear company," Mum offered by way of explanation, and to give Sarah time to collect herself.

"Lovely," she murmured. "Jo always did like nature."

"Truly awe-inspiring!" Bodey grinned broadly.

Aunt Jo beamed. I glanced up and saw a ripple of amusement cross Kane's features, but it immediately settled back into an expressionless mask. *OK, be miserable*, I thought to myself. *Suits me*. I could concentrate on using Bodey for flirting practice. But I would have to be subtle about it.

I didn't want Millie noticing. I'd never live it down.

Maisie was obsessed with flirting, and was forever reading out magazine articles to me on "How to get your Boy", but I'd never paid that much attention. Now I wished I'd shown a bit more interest. I tried hard to remember everything I could and made a list in my head:

1. Make as much eye contact as possible (without behaving like you're in a staring contest).

2. Laugh at everything remotely funny. If you're not sure if it's funny or not, play it safe and look fascinated instead.

3. Flick hair.

4. (Advanced.) As you are laughing at everything remotely funny, put your hand on his arm, as if to steady yourself.

That's as much as I could remember. It would have to be enough for now. I went through into the garden, feeling distinctly cheerful.

But that feeling didn't last long.

"I've put Mex, Bodey and Millie with us adults on the garden dining table. I'm afraid that you three younger ones will have to squash on to the little

table I've put on the end."

Mum must have noticed my expression because she said brightly, "So, we're all together really, aren't we?"

I observed the kiddies' table. It was significantly lower than the big one. And it was green plastic with ladybirds painted on the legs. I gave Mum a look, which she chose to ignore.

Cuba was whimpering about being starving and so didn't care where she sat just as long as someone put a burger in front of her soonish. Aunt Jo had tried very hard to make Cuba a vegetarian, but Cuba's inner spirit had apparently been reluctant to give up burgers.

She plonked herself down at the end and began frantically buttering a roll. This meant Kane and I had to sit opposite each other. He looked about as thrilled as I did as he contemplated the ladybirds. The good news was that Bodey was next to me, on the higher table, and I could still hear their conversation. And as Cuba was too busy shovelling food in her mouth, and Kane was too rude and unfriendly to speak to anyone, at least I could

enjoy Bodey's company and try out some of Maisie's flirting tips.

And I did. I didn't even have to pretend to laugh that much. Bodey had worked in a ski-hire shop all winter and had a hundred tales to tell about the tourists and their mad behaviour. I did find it difficult to keep flirty-giggling from becoming more hysterical-hyena, and Cuba complained I kept flicking my hair into her face, but I felt it was going well. Luckily, Millie was too busy talking to the grown-ups to notice what I was up to.

Just as I thought I could laugh no more, Bodey did a great imitation of Kane's face when he had gone into the ski shop one day and walked in on a girl in the changing rooms. "His face," Bodey cried. "The terror! He thought he was going to be arrested at least!"

"I was eleven years old," Kane responded, unamused.

"Well, Bodey, you're the one who could teach your brother a thing or two about girls, aren't you?" said their dad, Gerry, appearing at the table with another plate stacked with burgers. "Mr

Lucy

Charm here seems to have every girl in school after him. Now come and take over on the griddle for me. Man's gotta eat, you know!" Gerry laughed as he wiped his sweaty, red face with his apron and took his place at the head of the table.

I turned to Kane.

"Isn't your brother so funny?"

"Sure," he replied in a deadpan voice, without looking up. "I think he's the funniest guy in the whole world. No..." he paused, "the universe."

I looked at him sharply. "Well, there's no need to be sarcastic."

He lifted his head, and his dark-blue eyes shot a flash across the table.

"I'm not being sar-cas-tic." He mimicked my English accent. "I'm more than aware of my brother's mega-charm. You have to remember I live with it twenty-four seven. And er ... how long have you been here…?"

"Long enough to recognize someone with the manners to make an effort. Someone who is good company." It was my turn to flash my eyes across the table.

Kane leaned forward. "Well, it's very hard to be good company with a person who hasn't bothered to say a word to you since they sat down. Why don't you just clamber right up on to the next table? It's obviously where you want to be."

"What?!" I felt my face redden. Perhaps I hadn't been as subtle with the flirting thing as I'd hoped. "Well, yes, yes it is. It's not like you've made any effort to be friendly. Anyway, I think he is funny."

"Well I had noticed. I haven't heard cackling like that since I watched *The Wizard of Oz*."

"Pardon?!"

"You two!"

We both turned to glance at Cuba, who was now holding her fork halfway to her mouth, staring at us. "You're creating bad karma around me," she mumbled. "Can you both chill for a while?"

Another plate of burgers was brandished in front of us.

"Come on, you guys! Have some more." Bodey was leaning in next to his brother, grinning.

"Hope Kane's kept you entertained while I've been away," he said, winking at me before he went

off to serve the others. I was annoyed to find myself blushing again. I gathered myself and turned to Kane.

"You don't believe in making any effort at all with people, do you?" I observed.

"No point when I always have my terrific big brother Bodey to do it for me."

"Are you always like this?"

"Like what?"

"Like rude."

"I'm rude?! From the girl who just told me that I was boring!"

"I didn't exactly say that. I said you could make an effort. Try to be a bit more like your brother."

He stared pointedly at Millie. She had just finished saying something to Bodey and they were laughing. "And it's such a shame you're not more like your sister," he responded.

He tipped his chair back and rocked.

Neither of us spoke for several minutes. It was like high noon in a cowboy film. Cuba sighed and munched on — our bad karma thankfully not affecting her appetite.

"So," she sighed eventually, placing her knife and fork on her empty plate, "what is there to do around here, Kane?"

"Loads," Bodey interrupted cheerfully, as he sat down again. "Cycling, hiking, canoeing. The mountains are fantastic in summer. Don't waste your time asking Kane – unless you want to skateboard or sit alone on the lake."

"Lucy used to skateboard, didn't you?" Millie nodded in my direction. "You were always down at the skatepark with Lucas."

I gave her a cool look. I didn't want Bodey to know about my tomboy past. It didn't fit in with trying to be flirty, though by now I was so annoyed with Kane, I couldn't be giggly any more anyway. "That was ages ago," I muttered.

"Not that long ago. In fact, weren't you down at the skatepark last weekend? Lucy usually likes to do boy stuff," she explained. "Though you're acting very weird this evening." She rolled her eyes in the direction of Bodey. "Are you OK?"

"I don't only like to do boy stuff!" I yelled, embarrassed. "And skateboarding isn't necessarily

boy stuff anyway."

"Are you all right down there?" Mum called. "Lucy and Millie, you're not arguing, are you?"

We shook our heads and Mum went back to her conversation with Sarah.

"Of course skateboarding's not only for boys," Bodey said. "All the girls around here are down at the skatepark all the time. *Not.* Well, not the ones the boys are interested in, anyway."

"Maybe Lucy could go down there and show Kane how good she is," Millie suggested. She had a dangerous look about her – the one that says she's going to say something to make me mad. "Oh! But Kane – you'll have to behave yourself when you're alone with her."

"Millie!" I shrieked.

She pretended not to hear me. "Mmmm… The last time she was alone with a boy he lived to regret it."

"Millie, shut up!" Any last idea of being girly had flown out of the window. I wanted to kill her.

And now she was on a roll. "Happened just yesterday. This boy, Craig, who we met on

Vancouver Island ... he took a real shine to Lucy..."

I sat and seethed.

Bodey grinned. "So what happened?"

"He tried to kiss her. Last night. On the beach."

"And?"

"She slapped a handful of seaweed in his face, before knocking him flat on the rocks."

Everyone burst out laughing.

"You two sure are different, aren't you?" said Bodey.

I felt myself going scarlet. If I'd had some seaweed in my hand right then I'd have shoved it in Millie's face. How stupid of me to think that anyone would think of me as attractive when she was around.

Kane leaned forward. He fixed me with his intense blue eyes and paused for a moment before saying, "Isn't your sister *so* funny..."

War had been declared.

9

"You want to skateboard, Lucy?" Sarah placed a huge pile of warm pancakes down on the breakfast bar. "Really? We were all going to go shopping and then go for a swim in the outdoor pool down in the resort. Well, not Mex and Bodey, they're going fishing. Well, they will be when Bodey decides to get out of bed."

"I want to skateboard."

Mum gave me one of her "Why are you being so difficult?" looks.

The sun streamed through the picture windows

in the kitchen. Outside, the brilliant blue sky dropped behind the white and green of the huge mountains all around us.

When we had emerged from Rambling Rose earlier and wandered inside, Kane was already sitting at the breakfast bar. He was wearing a creased, blue cotton shirt over an old T-shirt and a pair of baggy jeans. He'd mumbled hello, and kept his eyes on his plate. Until now.

"Today's not a good day," he said, glaring at me. "There's a competition at the skatepark."

"Well, why can't you take Lucy along? She might like to watch?" Sarah replied, ignoring Kane's lethal stare.

I shrugged my shoulders. "I can skateboard."

"Well that's great! You'd be happy to take her, wouldn't you, Kane? She can ride my bike down there."

Kane stared at me, expressionless. I could only imagine his horror at the prospect of tomboy-girl tagging along when he met all his mates at the park. It made me all the more determined to go.

Bodey wandered into the kitchen and gave Millie

and me one of his dazzling smiles. I smiled back, trying to act as normal as possible. When we had got into our beds last night Millie had surprised me by saying quietly into the darkness, "You thought Bodey was pretty funny tonight, didn't you? Has my little sister got a crush?!"

I was glad she couldn't see me blush.

"He was funny!" I said defensively. "It seems to me I wasn't the only one who found him amusing. You were laughing, too," I huffed.

"But did you notice that he had to be the centre of attention the whole time? I know he's very charming, but he's really not that interested in other people unless it's to mock them. I bet he never lets Kane get a look-in."

"Kane doesn't want a look-in," I hissed. "Kane is rude and unfriendly. And as for mocking other people, after tonight, you can hardly talk, can you?"

I heard a deep sigh. "Whatever, Lucy, but take it from me. Bodey is all about Bodey."

I had stayed awake for a while thinking about what she had said and I'd realized that she was right – Bodey was only interested in himself. To be

honest, I'm not sure that he had even noticed me simpering and giggling like an idiot. But Kane had, and his words still stung. The least I could do to ease the humiliation was to annoy him today.

"It's not a good day," he repeated. "There's a competition."

"That's even better." I smiled back at him.

"OK," said Sarah. "Kane, go and dig out your old board and Bodey's helmet and pads. "Lucy can watch and she may be able to get some skateboarding in afterwards." She smiled. "Excellent. It's great to see you two getting along."

If only she knew.

"You'll ruin your clothes at that park," she continued, looking down at my too-small jeans. "It's so dusty. I've got an old pair of Kane's jeans he grew out of ages ago. They should fit you."

She went to fetch them and handed them over. I changed in Rambling Rose. The jeans fitted surprisingly well and they were long, too. The only problem was they sat on my hips and my pale-blue T-shirt was too short, exposing a few inches of stomach. I stood in front of the mirror and began

to drag my hair back into its usual untidy ponytail.

"Here, Lucy, let me." I turned in astonishment. Millie was standing behind me. "Let me do your hair. Give me a chance to tidy it up for once."

"I'm only going to the skatepark, Millie. You know, it's what us tomboys do!" I cried.

She snatched the hairbrush from my hand and slid the band off my ponytail. She began to brush my hair back from my face. "I know where you're going, but that's no reason to look such a mess."

After she had brushed it smooth and straight, she took the hair from the side of my face and drew it back into the band at the back, so it held out of my eyes. She viewed her handiwork.

"There, that's better."

"I'd better change this T-shirt," I mumbled, starting to pull it off.

"What are you doing?" she cried. "Leave it! You'll mess up your hair and I'm not doing it again. That T-shirt looks good with those jeans anyway."

"Does it?" I looked down. "I think it's too short."

"No it isn't, it looks cool, and your stomach is nice and brown now, show it off."

I stared at her. "I don't want to show anything off. I'm going skateboarding."

"Trust me, Lucy. The T-shirt's fine."

"Sure?"

"Sure."

"Why are you being so nice, Millie? You're scaring me."

"Don't be. I'm not doing it out of kindness to you. It's out of kindness to me. I can hide from your appearance at home, but now I have to live within a few feet of you at all times and I can't ignore it any more."

And I knew that was the nicest Millie was going to get. But it was something.

Back in the house Kane wordlessly handed me my knee and elbow pads and a helmet. We went to the garage and wheeled out the bikes, skateboards under one arm.

A loud wolf-whistle pierced the air. Bodey was pulling out of the driveway in his car. He leaned out of the window.

"Wow! Quite the foxy skater girl aren't you, Lucy? At least those boys will have something

pretty to look at at the skatepark."

I blushed.

"Well, are you coming or not?" Kane growled as Bodey and Mex set off in a scream of burning rubber.

I pulled myself together. "Sure. Lead the way."

We cycled along the road in the bright sunshine. Above us, the Rocky Mountains rose on all sides.

I knew that Kane wanted to say something to me; he kept coming alongside and then drifting forward and back. Eventually, he cleared his throat. "Er … about the skatepark?"

"Yes?"

"Well, I don't think it's like the one you go to in England."

"Why not?"

"Well, not many girls go to our one. It's a kind of boy thing. I mean girls come to watch, but not to actually … you know…"

"Skateboard?"

"That's right."

"Well, it's about time this place dragged itself into the twenty-first century and they did."

"It's just that some of the boys, they can be a bit … you might not like their sense of humour."

"You think they're going to laugh at me, do you?"

"They could…"

"I'm touched by your concern."

He sighed and concluded in an exasperated voice, "Well, don't say I didn't warn you. It's just today is not a good day. Seriously." He cycled angrily on in front of me. But the fact he was making it so obvious he didn't want me around made me all the more determined to stick to my plan.

When we arrived at the skatepark, a large group of boys were already practising jumps, sliding along the grind rail and rolling down the half-pipe. Above them on the grass, two girls were sitting on a long seat cut out of a log, enjoying the sunshine.

The large bowl where the skatepark was situated was dug out of the green parkland around it, and in the distance I could see children playing on shiny new swings and slides. There was no sign of the grim, grey concrete and the litter-strewn corners of the graffiti-covered park where Lucas and I hung out. This was big and clean and

Canadian, but I was determined not to show that I was impressed.

"Not a big competition, is it?" I observed. "Compared to the ones in England I'm used to."

Kane's eyes narrowed. "Just between ourselves. Local kids."

He slowed down as we approached. I could tell he wasn't looking forward to introducing me to his mates. We got off our bikes and wheeled them over to the log. One of the girls looked up. She had long, chestnut-brown hair, and was wearing denim shorts and a white halter-neck.

The other girl was smaller, with white-blonde hair, and dressed in a yellow T-shirt and black shorts. She was very pretty with huge, blue eyes and a small turned-up nose. She looked like a doll. She eyed me silently before sliding her eyes sideways and murmuring coyly, "Hiya, Kane."

"Tara." He nodded.

Both girls looked meaningfully at me, then back at Kane.

"This is, er ... Lucy. She's from England. She's staying for a few days."

Two pairs of eyes flicked from my head to my toes.

"Hi," I ventured.

"Hi! I'm Alex." The girl with the chestnut hair beamed at me. I smiled back.

Tara gave a tight, fake grin. "You're not going to skate, are you?"

I looked down at my pads and skateboard. "No, why would you think that?"

Alex laughed. "That was kind of an obvious question, Tara."

Tara scowled at her.

"It's just that most girls around here don't usually…" Alex explained.

A gang of the boys came wandering over. They were all looking curiously at me. I held my head up high and met their stares with a steady one of my own. I saw Kane watching the tallest – a red-headed boy. He walked right up to him, and the two boys squared up to one another.

"S'up, Kane."

"S'up, Paul," he replied. Paul jerked his head in my direction.

Lucy

"Lucy," Kane muttered in explanation. "From England. Staying for a couple of days. Wants to skateboard."

Paul grinned. "Serious? Solo's little English friend is gonna skate?"

I frowned. "Solo?"

Paul grinned. "That's what we call Kane, 'cos he likes to go off into the mountains all on his own and hang out where the wild things are!" Paul winked at me. "Kane here thinks he's gonna beat me today, don't ya?"

Kane looked him right in the eyes. "Maybe."

"Well, we'll soon find out, won't we? Let's get practising. Deal is whoever jumps the highest 360 on the half-pipe wins." He smirked at Tara. "And we all know what the prize is, don't we?"

Tara giggled and flashed a glance at Kane from under her eyelashes. Kane noticed but whatever he thought, his features gave nothing away. Anyone could see that Tara was one of those girls that boys go for in a big way. And she knew it.

However, now, no doubt because I was dressed to skate, the boys were all still looking at me.

I pretended not to notice and had a look at the half-pipe instead.

A half-pipe is exactly what it sounds like – as if someone has cut the most enormous pipe in two and laid the bottom piece in the ground. Boys were already sliding down one side and up the other, flipping their skateboards at the top and coming back down and up the other side again. A 360 meant they'd skate right up and off the pipe, turn their skateboards around a complete circle in mid-air, holding on to one end with one hand to control it, then land back down on the pipe again. Most of them couldn't do it and the air was full of clattering boards and curses.

I followed the group. Paul turned back to me. "People usually watch from here."

I gestured to my helmet and pads. "I don't want to watch. I want to skate."

He laughed again.

"No. Serious? You can't do the half-pipe. It's a 360 competition. You can skate when we've finished."

"Look," I said, realizing I needed to adjust the

Lucy

strap on my helmet. "I'll sit here for a bit and then come down, OK? When I've seen you do it then I'll have a better idea of what the standard is."

"Good idea!" Paul smiled. "Because we wouldn't want you to get hurt or anything."

There was a murmur of agreement from some of the boys. Kane frowned and began to say something to Paul.

"I'll be along in a minute then," I called.

Alex moved up on the log seat to make a space for me. The boys began to wander down the side of the bowl. I wanted to watch, but Tara and Alex turned themselves around in the opposite direction to lift up their faces to the sun.

"Don't you want to watch?" I asked, as I lifted my legs over the log.

"No, so boring," Tara sighed, her eyes momentarily closed. "I'm only gonna watch when Kane and Paul do the 360 thing."

"You've come on a really exciting day," Alex gushed. "Really exciting. It's like Kane and Paul are knights fighting for Tara's hand. No one's actually said it, but Tara's sort of let it be known that she

will go on a date with the winner."

Tara gave a smug smirk.

Alex continued. "It's so romantic. Tara just can't make up her mind – she's kept the two of them strung along for ages…"

"I haven't!" Tara smirked again. "It's so hard to commit to one of them, that's all. Kane's much better looking in that gorgeous, kinda intense way … but he's so busy thinking stuff all the time. He's not such a party animal as Paul. Paul's really popular and outgoing and everyone pays attention to him … don't they, Alex? But his problem is…"

"He can be kinda mean sometimes…" Alex offered.

"No! Not mean!" Tara said, annoyed. "I was going to say he's not as smart, like in class. No, Paul's not mean. He's funny. He's always playing jokes on people and making wisecracks. Sometimes people don't have a sense of humour about his teasing that's all."

"Sounds to me like the class clown," I said, "but with a crass sense of humour."

Tara's mouth fell open.

A low voice interrupted our conversation. "Well, isn't it lucky I don't care what your opinion is."

I whipped around. It was Paul, standing behind me, with Kane next to him.

"What are you doing creeping up on us like that!" Tara shrieked.

"Sorry." He stared at me. "Your friend Kane says that we should give you a go on the half-pipe."

"Well, that's very kind of him," I said slowly, "but this is a public skatepark and I don't need Kane or anyone else's permission to skate, thank you. And another thing. I'm entering the competition."

"You can't," Paul snapped.

"Let her have a go," Kane said calmly. "If she's so mad keen to do it, why not let her? She says she can skateboard, bugged me all morning to get here. If she can't cut it that's her problem."

Paul glared at him.

"You're not scared, are you?" I gave Paul a level stare.

He burst out laughing. "You kidding! You! Beat me on a skateboard. Never in a million years."

"If I jump a higher 360 than you – what will

I win?" I asked.

"I can't be messing with this. You see, Lucy, it's, er … not like a normal competition. I mean what would you win?" Paul gave Tara a wink and began to turn and walk away.

I called after him. "If I win, I want you to say to me, 'You're a better skateboarder than me, Lucy McDonnell.' That's all."

"Yeah right," he murmured. "Like that's gonna happen. Let's get on with this."

I got up and followed them down to the half-pipe. So did Tara. By now a large gang had gathered.

"Let her skate."

"Yeah, what are you afraid of?"

Paul cast an eye over his audience. They stared back at him. He shrugged. "OK, then. Whatever."

There was a murmur of approval.

"Who's going first?" I asked, when we got up to the edge of the half-pipe.

"Pull straws," Paul suggested. Tara had followed us. She ripped a piece of paper from her pocket into three different-sized strips.

Lucy

"Longest one goes first," she instructed.

Paul got the longest, I got the next one and Kane the shortest.

"Go Paul!" Tara yelled half-heartedly. Paul rocked to and fro on the edge, psyching himself up. Then he launched himself off and thundered up the other side. He lifted himself into the air and did a perfect 360, crashing down on to the half-pipe and triumphantly coming to a halt up on the other side.

"Beat that!" he crowed.

I had been warming up by gently rolling up and down the half-pipe. It felt good to be back on a skateboard, but I wasn't going to give anything away just yet. I knew I was good. Being on a skateboard came as naturally to me as breathing. I skated to the top of the half-pipe and balanced my board on the edge. Every single person who had been skateboarding elsewhere in the park had come over to watch. I stared back at them.

"Well, take a look at this, Canada!" I said to myself, as I tipped my skateboard over the edge and launched myself down the half-pipe. I flew

down the pipe, slammed up the other side and hurled myself into the air. I span around. My hand steadied the end of the board and I felt the familiar thrill, as if I was flying. I knew before I touched solid ground again that I had jumped higher than Paul. I kept my focus as I crashed back down the side and rumbled back up the other one to a sharp, snappy stop. I kicked up my skateboard into my hand and took off my helmet.

Everyone stared at me for a moment. Then they began to cheer.

I caught Kane's eye. To my surprise, he was smiling at me, and to my even greater amazement I couldn't stop myself smiling back. *Not bad for a tomboy, hey?* I thought to myself.

"Your turn now, Kane," Tara snapped, stepping in between us.

Kane picked up his skateboard.

"Good luck!" she cried, never taking her eyes off him. At the top of the half-pipe he stopped. He had a serious look about him, like he was deciding something. At the final moment his eyes caught mine again, then he tipped down off the edge of

the half-pipe and hurled himself down the side and up the other one. His jump was good, really good, but I could see immediately what Tara and Paul already knew – that it wasn't as good as mine. Kane rolled back towards us on his board, shrugging his shoulders.

"Guess you won," he said, as he came to a halt in front of me. "Congratulations." I said nothing.

The two boys judging ran up. They'd decided to call second place a draw between Kane and Paul.

"Wow, that was so cool!" Alex gasped. "You're amazing! You could go professional!"

Tara said nothing. I knew she was angry. I'd messed up her moment. And girls like Tara didn't like that.

Paul was sloping off. I called out. "Hey! Don't you have something to say to me?"

Paul scowled and continued to walk away.

"What a bad loser." I tut-tutted. "Time for me to go, I think."

"Hey, don't go yet!" one of the judges shouted.

"Yeah, stay." And then they were all saying it.

I looked at the group of boys around me, but I'd

made my point. I was ready to leave. "No, I've got to get back." Kane picked up his skateboard as if to come with me. Tara's face fell.

"You don't have to come back too, Kane," I said. "I can remember the way."

"No, better come with you; my mom would kill me if you got lost or something."

"You don't have to … I know the way."

"I'm coming, OK!" he yelled.

"Whoa. OK then. No need to shout."

"Yeah, no need to be a sore loser," one of the boys yelled.

As we cycled back I drew alongside him on my bike.

"Why did you do that?"

"Do what?"

"Let me win. I saw you on the pipe in your garden, you can jump higher than me. Why did you let me beat you? I don't get it."

He gave me a wry smile.

"Guess I had a few reasons."

"Go on."

"First, I couldn't resist seeing Paul's face if you

were good. He's such a jerk about girls and I wanted to see how he'd react if you beat him."

"But what if I hadn't been good? You didn't know what I could do?"

Kane nodded.

"But then you would have made a fool of yourself and that would have been entertaining for me…"

I gave him a sharp, sideways glance.

"Seriously…" he continued swiftly, "at first I thought you were only saying you wanted to come to the park to bug me, which it did, but on the way here I got to thinking, and I guessed a girl like you wasn't going to risk falling flat on her face in front of a bunch of strangers, however annoying she finds me."

I couldn't resist smiling. "And secondly?"

He cycled on for a while before answering. "Just decided it wasn't that important to win."

"Really? And why was that?"

"Maybe realized the prize wasn't so interesting after all."

"Seriously? I would have thought any boy would

think a date with Tara was quite a prize."

He sighed. "Naaah. It was a dumb idea right from the start. I can't believe I bought into it."

"What if she chooses you, though? The judges said it was a draw between you and Paul so she can choose between you."

He laughed. "Those boys who did the judging have both experienced Paul's 'sense of humour' in the past. I'll get them to say that after careful deliberation they feel that Paul just had the edge on me. I agreed to the competition more to teach him a lesson rather than get a date with Tara. When I think about it she's *so* not my type."

"And what is your type?" I asked without thinking.

Suddenly he was staring straight into my eyes, and I don't know what happened, but my bike wobbled, I hit the grass bank and the next thing I knew I was lying in a ditch.

"Kane and Lucy have to go together."

We both looked at the canoe. I wondered if Kane felt as uncomfortable about that arrangement as I did. Ever since that look from him on the way back from the skatepark the day before, it was not just the spokes on my bike that were whirling. My emotions were in a spin, too.

For the first time in my life a boy was having an effect on me that I was finding hard to control. Kane had reached out a hand to haul me up out of the ditch, but I was so flustered that instead of

simply playing it cool and saying thank you, I started to babble with embarrassment, and for the rest of the journey I'm sure I had talked complete rubbish.

All I could think about was that look. What had it meant? Maybe I had read it wrong. I needed to get a grip before I made a total fool of myself. Again.

What was the matter with me? I was either stuffing seaweed in people's faces or falling off bikes when they so much as looked me in the eyes. I wished Maisie was here. If I could've talked it over with her, I knew she'd help me work out what it all meant, even if it was that I was imagining things.

Without her advice to guide me, I decided that the best thing to do was hide my feelings, but that has never been my strong point, so when we got back I pretended that I felt dizzy after the fall and went to lie down in Rambling Rose. Mum had tried to persuade me to eat with everyone else, but I'd told her I wasn't hungry.

Now we were both standing outside the bleached wooden boathouse on the edge of the dazzling blue water of Lake McGillivray, about to share a canoe. And I couldn't help thinking that it seemed like the

perfect place to embarrass myself again.

The huge, bearded man who was handing out the life jackets had insisted that no one could go in a canoe without an experienced canoeist. All the Canadian boys were, of course. Even Mex paddled off with his cooked-spaghetti arms like he was born on the water.

Cuba wanted to go with her brother and then I just knew what would happen with the last two canoes. Millie and Bodey were the same age, so that was it. I was with Kane.

As he hauled on his life jacket and pulled the straps tight, I couldn't possibly guess what he thought about the prospect of spending another day with me. I had lain awake last night going over the incident on the bike and *that* look. In the end, I'd decided that I was going to act ordinary, and treat him like anyone else, no one special. Like someone who hadn't started to make my heart beat faster when I saw him at breakfast this morning, or made it difficult for me to concentrate on anything else when he stood near me.

Together, the three canoes set off from the

boathouse on to the water. It took me a while to get settled, and get to grips with the paddle, but Kane was in no mood to be patient. He picked at every move I made – I was sitting too much on one side, I was dipping my paddle at the wrong angle… I breathed a sigh of relief – acting like I wasn't keen on him might prove easier than I had imagined. He could be so annoying. Perhaps I didn't like him after all.

We paddled out on to the icy water, with the mountains reflected on the lake's glassy surface. I was overcome with the stillness of the scene as the shoreline drifted further and further away.

Well, I would have been if Kane hadn't been so bad-tempered.

"Don't hold the paddle that way! Hold it this way!" he snapped, looking round.

"I am holding it *this way*!" I yelled back, raising it in the air with both arms and shaking it.

He glanced behind him again. "No you're not. Look at me, see how I do it. Then do the same."

I watched his back as he cut strong, clean strokes through the water, forgetting to join in with

my own paddle.

"Jeez. What are you doing now, Lucy? Do I have to paddle by myself?"

I jumped. I'd been totally mesmerized. "Er, nothing … I just thought I'd get a sandwich out, for later." I scrambled behind me for my backpack.

"For goodness' sake, we've only been in the water five minutes. Stop rocking the canoe and start paddling." He raised his oar. "This way. Come on!"

"OK! Just let me put my backpack away."

"Sure. But here's an idea – try and make some time in your busy canoe-jobs schedule to paddle. And then you might get to appreciate some of the most beautiful scenery you'll ever see."

"You'll be grateful I got that sandwich out later," I muttered.

"Now I know why I always prefer to come here alone," he said through gritted teeth.

That stung.

"Look, I'm trying my best. I've never done this before."

"That's obvious. But if you could actually admit, just once in your life, that someone knows better

than you, it would be a help."

"If you weren't such an impatient, moody teacher I might learn faster."

"Me? Moody! That's a joke. Coming from you."

I flushed with irritation. "Look, I'm sorry you've got to hang out with me. I know you'd rather be on your own. I'm making a huge effort to be pleasant here."

"So this is you being pleasant, is it? I'd hate to see you being unpleasant. Oh, wait a minute. I have seen that, haven't I? The first night you arrived in fact…"

I couldn't believe it. We'd only been alone a short while and we were fighting already. This wasn't what I'd hoped for, but still I couldn't stop myself continuing the war of words.

"Well, if you were more like your brother, people might like you better."

"If you were more like your sister, people might like you better."

"You really haven't grown up at all since we last visited all those years ago, have you?"

He turned around to frown at me, then turned

back shaking his head. "And you, you're still a total pain in the—"

"Hey, you two!" It was Bodey and Millie, effortlessly slipping through the water towards us. "Stop with the yelling. You'll be scaring away every wild animal for miles."

Kane turned around to give me an "I told you so" glare that succeeded in reducing me to silence. I began to paddle in time with him. I wanted to hold on to my anger – it was easier to deal with than the new emotions I'd been feeling.

After a while, I began to fall under the spell of the Rockies and the soothing splash, splash of the oars. Kane began to grudgingly point out birds and wildlife. An eagle skimming the lake to catch a fish. An elk moving through the pines in the forest.

The other two canoes drifted out of sight ahead of us, and after a while Kane stopped paddling and I followed his lead. He didn't have to tell me why, it was so we could feel the silence. I was very aware of him sitting calmly in front of me, staring out ahead. I didn't feel calm, though; I felt a tension in the air crackling around me and I

knew I was blushing. I forced myself to breathe normally and relax. After a while, he turned around.

"What do you think of it?"

I told the truth. "I love it. It's so beautiful and peaceful."

Kane nodded.

"And when you've been living within a few feet of other people for a while I can't tell you how good it feels to be alone..." I blushed. "Well, not alone..."

"I know, you don't have to explain. That's why I come out here."

There was another small silence.

"I'm sorry," I said.

"What for?"

"Being a pain."

He grinned. "Well, I guess we're both good at that. Better make up some time, I suppose." He dipped his paddle in the water. "C'mon. Get paddling."

But I didn't want to move. I just wanted to stay there with him, caught in the moment.

Suddenly Kane stopped again and reached back

Lucy

with a warning touch on the back of my hand. With his other hand he pointed at the shore. A small, black bear had lumbered down to the shoreline and was standing on a rock, watching the water.

"He's looking for fish," Kane whispered, his body tense. You couldn't help but be impressed by the bear's very presence. There was an air of quiet assurance in his movements.

I remembered my promise to Maisie. I knew now wasn't the time, but I had promised.

"I'm going to have to take a photo," I whispered.

"What, now?! Do you have to?"

I began to rummage in my bag. "I'm sorry, but I promised my friend."

"I promised my friend." He mimicked my voice. "Do you do everything your friends tell you to do?"

"No, but that's not the point. You live here. It's OK for you, you probably see a bear every week, but some of us may never see this again."

"Couldn't you just buy a postcard? A photo will be useless. He'll just be a dot from here."

I knew he was right, but I had the camera in my hand by now and I had promised. "I'll just take one."

I held on to the side of the canoe to balance myself as I stood up.

"What are you doing?" Kane hissed.

"I can get a better shot without your big head in the way."

"Sit down!"

"No! It won't take a moment."

"Just sit down, will you?"

Why was he being such a control freak?

I began to rock the canoe from side to side. "Look, it's quite stable, you're not scared, surely? And stop telling me what to do. If I want to take a photo or rock this boat I will," I protested.

"Sit down!" He lunged for the camera and I reared back in surprise. The camera clattered to the floor of the canoe and my arms flailed about as I lost my balance and tipped backwards into the lake.

There is no water as cold as water that's come from a melted glacier. It was like jumping into a bath of ice cubes. Just as I thought I was going to die, my life jacket bobbed me up to the surface. Kane's arms reached out and dragged me, like a sack of potatoes, over the side of the canoe.

When he had established that I was alive, he immediately abandoned me in a heap and began to row furiously to a small island a short distance ahead. I raised my head over the side – back on the shoreline, the bear had gone.

"Why did you do that?" I shouted, through chattering teeth.

"Oh yes, it's my fault, isn't it?" he yelled back, without turning round. "My fault you had to take a photo when I asked you not to. My fault when I told you not to stand up but you did anyway. Of course it is. My fault that you fell in and look like..." He turned around and stared at me. I scowled angrily back. "...Like an irritated seal..." He turned to face the front again, but I could see by the way his shoulders were moving that he was laughing. Laughing! I could have died in that lake and he was laughing. By the time he hauled the canoe up on to the beach, I was shivering all over and my fingers were turning blue. He chucked my backpack at me. "Get changed quickly, you need to warm up."

I marched off towards the pines to find

some privacy.

"Hey, Lucy," he yelled after me. "You've, er ... got something stuck to your bum."

I reached round and peeled a soggy sandwich off the back of my shorts with as much dignity as I could. Then I stuck my nose in the air and stomped off.

After I had taken off my wet things and changed into dry shorts and a fleece, I felt better but still freezing. I emerged from the trees and sat on a rock, shivering and hugging my knees. I put my head in my arms. The day had been a disaster. I don't know how I could ever have imagined us getting on together. I didn't even care that he'd laughed at me when he'd dragged me out of the water. I didn't like him anyway. In fact, I hated him.

I felt a twig prod my leg. "Get up."

"Go away."

"Get up, you're still cold, you need to run around and get your circulation going."

I lifted my head. "You are kidding?"

The twig prodded again. I put my head back in my arms and ignored it.

Lucy

"Move."

"No."

"Don't force me to make you."

"Oh yeah? Like, how are you going to do … ouch!"

He gave an extra sharp prod. I snatched my foot away.

"I'm doing this for your own good, Lucy. You don't think I like doing it, do you?"

"Ouch! Stop it." I was halfway on to my feet now, but suddenly finding it hard not to giggle.

He prodded me again. "I'll bet you run like a girl, don't you? I bet you can't get to that tree over there and back to the canoe without me catching you."

I looked up and measured the distance. I paused. Then I looked over his shoulder.

"Is that a bear?" I gasped.

He turned and I was up and running across the beach in a flash.

Although I was fast, I knew he was a lot faster, but as I hurtled around the woods twice and three times around the little cove, he kept just behind me. Eventually I flopped, laughing too much

to run another step, into the canoe. He collapsed in after me.

I gasped, "You let me win. Again!"

"Warmer now?" he asked.

"Much."

"Let me see. Give me your hands."

We sat facing each other on the seats. He reached out to take my hands in his. I felt the warmth of his fingers holding on to mine. I looked up into his dark-blue eyes. They had the same expression in them that had sent me falling into a ditch the day before. This time though, I held his gaze.

11

"Yoooo hoooo!"

The call carried clear as a bell across the water. Our hands jerked apart.

In the distance we could see two canoes paddling swiftly towards us.

"What have you guys been doing?" Cuba yelled, as she got closer. "We've had to come back to find you AGAIN."

"I fell in," I explained.

She stared at me. "How on earth did you manage that?"

I looked at Kane. "I stood up in the boat to take a photo of a bear and I lost my balance."

Cuba did one of her tut-tuts. "How dumb was that? You OK?"

I found myself smiling. "I'm fine now."

"That is so typical of you." Millie paddled up with Bodey. She turned to Kane. "I bet you tried to tell her not to and she wouldn't listen?"

Kane grinned.

"I knew it. When will you ever learn to listen to other people?" Millie sighed. "But at least you're all right. Well, now we're all here let's eat. I'm starving."

And I realized that I was, too. We pulled the canoes up out of the water and sat down. Everyone began to unload sandwiches, fruit cake and chocolate bars from their backpacks. I don't know whether it was the blue sky, the mountains or the lake but as we all sat there in the sunshine it tasted like the best picnic I had ever had.

"Come on then," Bodey said after we had cleared up every scrap. "You two can lead the way," he added, looking over at me and Kane.

"We're not letting you out of our sight from now on. We don't want any more accidents."

As we paddled back out into the water, I couldn't help grinning to myself. It had been one of the best days of my life. I hadn't had to be flirty or laugh in a fake way, or twiddle my hair, I had just been myself. And Kane had seemed to like me, exactly as I was; with my old, worn-out clothes, messy hair and un-made-up face. I could hardly believe it, but I really hoped I was right, because one thing was for sure, I liked him, too.

That evening after supper, we had gone down to the half-pipe and messed about attempting to outdo each other for a while. Eventually we had flopped on to the grass and talked about our lives, our families and what it was like having super-confident older siblings like Bodey and Millie.

"That's why I didn't have much to say, you know, when you first got here," he explained. "Bodey always takes over when he's around; everyone always thinks he's so great, so I've sort of got into

thinking 'Why bother? Leave him to it.' But what annoys me is when you've been around him as long as I have, you realize that it's all so phoney. I hear him say the same stuff all the time. He likes being the centre of attention. I hate it. But you certainly seemed to think he was pretty great that first night ... though not so much this evening, I noticed."

I blushed. "Um, that first night was a bit weird. He was funny, but perhaps not quite as funny as I made out. I'd rather just forget it."

"I'm sorry I laughed when your sister told that story about you."

"I'm sorry I laughed when Bodey told that story about you. It wasn't even that funny."

"I know." He grinned at me. "But actually that seaweed story really was." I threw my jumper at him. He caught it in one hand. "So what was wrong with Craig?" he asked.

"What was wrong with Tara?" I responded.

"I told you. She's not my type."

"And what is your type? Someone who doesn't think Bodey is great?"

Lucy

"No. Though that would definitely help. I want someone I can connect with, talk to. Someone I can trust with stuff."

I found myself blushing furiously and turned away – could he be talking about me?

"I can't do all that fake charm talk," Kane said. "Maybe Bodey's right, maybe I should lighten up. But you know, the way I feel about things and the way people feel about me ... I take that seriously." He turned to face me. "It's too important. Does that sound crazy?"

"Lucy, Kane. Time to come in!" Aunt Jo's booming voice carried across the lawn.

Kane gave a start, and his dark-blue eyes flashed a smile at me. "Hey! You are dangerously easy to talk to. Not like most girls..."

I frowned. "You mean I'm like a boy?"

He threw back his head and laughed. "No, no way! And now I definitely should stop talking."

I heard Mum calling me from the house. I looked at my watch and wondered where the time had gone. It was late.

"See you tomorrow then." I smiled.

"Sure." He looked me straight in the eyes and smiled back.

A short while later, I was in my narrow bed with the curtain open, looking at the stars. Mum and Aunt Jo were finishing a bottle of wine in the garden with Sarah. Millie and Cuba were fast asleep, exhausted after a day of hard physical activity.

But I couldn't sleep. I was feeling happy in a way that I had never experienced before. And I knew the reason why. This time I was sure that I didn't need Maisie to tell me that I had read the signals right.

I heard a clatter outside Rambling Rose. It sounded like someone was putting the rubbish out. A mobile ringtone jarred the silence with its tinny tune. The night air clearly carried Bodey's voice.

"Yo, Judd. How's it going? No, no, not till tomorrow. Got the English crew staying till midday, I'll catch you after then. Let's meet at the diner. No? Why? Your sister's going there on a date with Kane? No way! Tara's going on a date with my kid brother? Seriously? The dog! What? No, no nothing. Just an expression. OK, we'll meet at Joe's instead, see ya!"

He cackled with laughter. "Well, well, well. So my little brother has a date! Maybe I've taught him something after all…"

I heard his footsteps head back towards the house.

Humiliation and anger flooded my veins in equal measure. Everything Kane said to me – had it all been lies? All that stuff about liking girls to be just who they are and not being fake … and now he was going on a date with Tara? But why had he said those things? Was it all a joke?

I'd been dreading leaving tomorrow. I'd imagined he might be feeling the same. All that excitement, all those good feelings – they didn't mean anything. He probably couldn't wait for me to go. Well, OK then. I'd show him that I couldn't care less about him either. But although I kept saying it to myself, the tears streamed down my face. I buried my head in my pillow so no one would hear me cry.

12

"Are you all right, Lucy?" Mum was looking at me in that way mums do. Aunt Jo and Cuba had already gone over to the house for breakfast.

"Fine," I said briskly, as I pulled my hair back into its old messy ponytail. I was back in my too-short jeans and an old T-shirt. I saw my red, puffy eyes reflected in the mirror. "Got a touch of hay fever, I think."

Millie looked up from where she still lying in bed. "Do you want me to—"

"No!" I snapped, tugging at the hairband.

She raised her eyebrows in surprise, then shrugged. "Whatever."

In the kitchen, I sat down as far away as possible from Kane and I gave his obviously fake smile an icy glare. He drew back, looking surprised. *I'll bet you're surprised*, I thought. *You think I still believe all those lies you told me yesterday. I know you're off to see Tara the minute I've gone. You think I'm some stupid girl who thinks you're great. Well I'm going to show you how little I care.*

He leaned forward to say something but I leaped up to put my plate in the dishwasher. He got up and followed me.

"You all right?"

I tossed my head. "Yes. Why wouldn't I be?"

"Well, it's just that you seem kind of…"

"Kind of what?"

He paused for a moment before continuing.

"I was only going to ask if you wanted to come down to the skatepark. It's your last morning, thought it might be fun – we could … talk."

"No thanks. I'd rather go shopping with Mum, Millie and Cuba."

"Really?" He sounded surprised. "Didn't think that was your thing at all."

"Well it is!" I snapped. "Anyway, I'm sure you've got your own busy schedule today." I threw the tea towel on to the hook and walked out. I could feel his eyes boring into me, but I didn't turn round.

As the morning in town dragged on, all I could think about was Kane.

"What's the matter with you, Lucy? Are you going to buy them?" Millie growled at me. We were in a clothes shop and Mum had agreed to get me some new jeans as Millie had pointed out that my old ones were practically Bermuda shorts. Millie had then picked out a white shirt which tied at the front. It fitted perfectly.

Any other day I would have considered it a good morning, but not that one. How had I got things so wrong? I thought about that first look, cycling back from the skatepark. I remembered him holding my hands in the canoe and last night, talking in the garden. Was it all in my imagination?

By the time we arrived back at the house it was lunchtime, and Sarah had planned a special farewell feast. I was hoping that Kane would have disappeared off to the skatepark, but he was sitting at the kitchen table, cradling a glass of juice. He looked up when I came in, but I pretended not to notice.

As we sat down to eat, I kept my eyes on my plate and tried to let the conversation wash over me. Kane was sitting opposite me trying to catch my eye, but he could save his meaningful looks for Tara.

"Don is going to be bowled over when he sees you in that dress," Aunt Jo beamed at Cuba. We'd spent about an hour trailing around every shop in town to find Cuba's perfect dress. It was a tight, purple mini and in my eyes it looked awful on her, but then again, what did I know about fashion? I was a skater girl. Boys clearly didn't go for my look.

"Don sounds pretty perfect," Bodey said with a grin. "The rest of us boys don't stand a chance, do we? What do you think, Millie?"

"I have Finn and he's perfect for me," she replied firmly. "I think everyone's idea of perfect is

different, and there's someone out there for everyone, even you, Lucy!" She gave me a wicked grin. "I mean look at us two, and you and Kane – totally different. Thank goodness."

"So true," Bodey agreed. "I'm good-looking and charming, and Kane is well, let's just say 'not'… Now which one of us would you date, Lucy?"

I forced a smile and pretended to be thinking. I could feel Kane's eyes boring into me but I knew now it was nothing to do with me. He was only jealous of Bodey. All the hurt and anger boiled up inside me.

I looked up and stared straight at Bodey. "You. By a mile."

Bodey slapped the table and hooted with delight. "Knew it!" he yelled triumphantly. "Yet again I conquer! Never mind, Kane, one day…"

And then I did catch Kane's eye and his expression was as blank as the first time I'd met him in the garden. He got up from the table and coolly wandered out of the room.

Millie grabbed my arm as soon as we'd finished lunch and climbed aboard Rambling Rose.

Lucy

"What the hell was that all about?"

I shook her arm off. "What do you mean?"

"You know what I mean. What happened with Kane? Yesterday you were both getting on like a house on fire. Today you're acting like you can't bear to be in the same room as him."

"You've got it completely wrong, Millie. I can't stand him. I hate him more this time than the last visit. He's a rude, hypocritical snake…"

"Oh, come on…" Millie wailed.

She saw the expression on my face.

"Oh, OK then, have it your way, but you haven't been chucking seaweed around again, have you?"

I began to angrily shovel clothes into drawers and bang them shut.

"No I haven't – but thanks for bringing that up again, Millie."

"And you didn't push him over on to any rocks causing him great pain and humiliation?"

I spun round and lunged towards her. "Look, it wasn't my choice to spend the day in that canoe with Kane yesterday – I would much rather have gone with any of the rest of you. And if you really

want to know it was the most dull and boring day of MY LIFE!"

Millie's eyes were looking fixedly over my shoulder. I looked round. Kane was framed in the doorway.

"Kane!" Millie cried. "Looking for something?"

"I was. But ... hey," he held my gaze, "it doesn't matter now." He turned his face away and disappeared back down the steps.

"Oh dear." Millie pulled a face. "That was pretty harsh, Lucy."

"He deserved it," I muttered, suddenly feeling like I was about to cry.

Millie shook her head. "I really don't understand you. What could he have possibly done to deserve that? I'm going back to the house to get my shopping." And she stomped off.

Above my head I heard a long, low whistle. I looked up. Cuba was lying on her bunk with her hands clasped behind her head. "Well, you've sure blown it now. That's a boy who won't forget you in a hurry. And not in a good way. What's the matter with you?"

"Nothing's the matter with me. He's the horrible one. He's the one who has been a big fake. He's the one who pretended to be all honest and truthful – but as soon as we're out of here, he's going off on a date with a … a … Barbie Doll!"

"What are you talking about?" Cuba peered over the side of her bunk. "What Barbie Doll?"

"I don't want to talk about it." I threw the last shirt in a drawer and banged it shut.

"You don't mean Tara, do you?"

My mouth dropped open in astonishment.

"How do you know about Tara?"

"Mex told me."

"Mex spoke to you!" I gasped.

Cuba gave me a level stare. "Just because we're not yelling and screaming at each other all the time like you and Millie, doesn't mean we never have a conversation."

"And what did he say?" I asked.

"You know he's been sharing Bodey's room? Well, he told me that last night Tara's brother, Judd, phoned Bodey and told him Tara was going on a date with Kane today."

"I know," I said grimly.

"How do you know?"

"I heard the conversation – he was outside on the mobile."

"But Lucy, you don't know the whole story. Mex was there when Judd phoned again this morning. He was mad with Kane. Apparently Tara had said there was a date – told the whole of Sun Peaks there was a date – only problem was, she forgot to tell Kane. Obviously didn't occur to her there might be a problem. And when she remembered to phone Kane this morning with the details he said a great big NO. So there you go – your 'Act first, think later' personality has got you into trouble again. You really should—"

But I didn't hear her last words. I dashed out of the door, through the house, into the back garden, and then back to where Sarah was standing on the driveway.

"Do you know where I can find Kane?" I asked breathlessly.

"Sorry, Lucy. I don't know where he's gone, either skateboarding or down by the lake, I expect.

Lucy

I'm afraid he's going to miss saying goodbye to everyone, but that's Kane for you. I can pass on a message?"

I shook my head dumbly. Cuba was right. If I had only kept my cool and thought things through I could have just asked Kane what was going on. Now I had managed to ruin everything. I couldn't leave without him knowing why I'd behaved like I had.

"Well come on then, time to go," Mum said, hugging Sarah. I could see she was feeling very sad about saying goodbye to her friend and didn't want to prolong the agony. Aunt Jo was edging her green, floral smock into the driver's seat.

"Come on, Lucy, get in," Mum urged. Aunt Jo started the engine and Rambling Rose spluttered into life.

"Mum," I whispered desperately.

"What is it?"

"All aboard!" yelled Aunt Jo, tooting the horn.

"Lucy?" Mum was looking at me anxiously now.

I looked down the long and empty road and willed Kane to appear. But apart from the trees dancing in the breeze and a cat sauntering across

the pavement, the road remained empty.

"Lucy? Is anything the matter?"

I shook my head. "No, I'm fine, it's nothing."

"Well come on, get in then."

I climbed the steps.

She shut the door behind me. Bodey and Sarah began to wave frantically, as Aunt Jo began reversing Rambling Rose down the driveway.

"Don't leave it another seven years!" Sarah called.

My stomach lurched. Would it be that long before I saw Kane again? I pressed my face against the glass and stared out. Tears pricked my eyes, but I didn't want to cry in front of Mum – she was already giving me concerned glances.

Cuba gave me a nudge. "Forget about him, Lucy. Bodey really was the more fun one."

I gave her a shocked stare and turned away. I knew that out of all the bad situations I'd got myself into in the past, none of them came close to being as awful as this one.

The only thing I could think about on the journey was that every mile that passed took me a mile further from Kane. Millie and Mum kept staring at me so I tried to look as normal as possible and pretended to concentrate on the scenery, which was becoming more and more dramatic as we climbed higher into the Rockies. We stopped for lunch at a roadside diner but I wasn't hungry.

"If you push that chip around your plate one more time it will sue you for harassment," Millie sighed. "You've hardly eaten a thing."

"Are you sure you're OK?" Mum asked. "You've been awfully quiet today."

"Don't worry, Clemmie," Aunt Jo said, smiling. "I'm sure she'll feel much better tonight."

We all looked at her. What was she on about? Aunt Jo gave us a mysterious look and laughed. "No, I'm not saying another word. We'll be there soon enough…"

A few hours later she swung Rambling Rose off the road and through two ornate iron gates and down a wide driveway that cut through a forest.

"Jo?" Mum said. "Where on earth…?"

"Just you wait and see…" Aunt Jo chuckled. "Ah yes … there it is."

We emerged from the pines and found ourselves facing what looked like an enormous palace on the edge of a huge, turquoise lake. With the towering mountains behind it, it looked like something out of a fairy tale.

Aunt Jo beamed. "Welcome to the Chateau Hotel on Lake Louise, one of the most beautiful hotels in the world. I know Mom gave you the money for one of those grand modern motorhomes, but

because I organized Rambling Rose, I took the liberty of spending the difference on a night of luxury along the way. We're in the best rooms, all with balconies overlooking the lake."

Aunt Jo turned to look at me. "I said you might feel better tonight, Lucy. Whatever problems you think you might have, I'm sure a night here couldn't fail to lift your spirits."

I smiled back. It was a treat, an amazing treat. The least I could do was show I was grateful.

A porter showed us to our room. He pushed open the door and Millie gasped. It was enormous, decorated in cream, pale blue and gold. Against one wall were two king-size beds, with about twenty oversize linen pillows on each, and on the other a large plasma TV. Two tall French windows, their long curtains softly billowing in the evening breeze, led out on to our balcony. As soon as the porter had gone, Millie yelped and jumped straight on to one of the beds. She lay on her back and made angel shapes, staring at the ceiling.

"It's huge! And it's all mine!"

Before I could say a word she had jumped up

and ran to investigate the bathroom. There was a loud echoing shriek from inside. "There's a jacuzzi in the bath, and you can sit in it and see the lake through the balcony windows. I can't wait; I've proved my pioneering spirit living in Rambling Rose, and now I'm going to have the biggest, longest soak in the world."

The bathroom door banged shut. I looked around me. It really was luxurious, it was just a shame that I wasn't in the mood to enjoy it properly. I went and sat on the balcony and watched the sun setting in pinks and golds over the mountains. I wondered what Kane was doing.

Eventually I heard the bathroom door open, disturbing my thoughts. I turned and saw a very pink Millie, wrapped in a huge white, fluffy bathrobe twisting a large towel around her head.

"Your turn now," she called out, moving swiftly around the room, opening and closing cupboards. "Come and look, Lucy."

I wandered back into the room and she pointed at her latest discovery. "There's a mini-bar, it's got juice, Coke, lemonade, anything you want. Like one?"

Lucy

I shook my head and sat down on the edge of my bed. She immediately plonked herself down on hers, opposite me.

"What's going on, Lucy? It's not about Bodey, is it? Because honestly, I told you, he's an attention-seeking jerk and he's too old for you anyway." She opened her can of lemonade. "So, what happened with you and Kane? He seemed to really like you."

I stared fixedly at the floor.

But Millie hadn't finished. "You can't be all smiling and laughing one minute and then all weird and mean the next, you know…"

My fingers gripped the edge of the bedcover tightly to stop myself crying.

"…I mean, was that day on the lake with Kane really the most dull and boring day of your life?"

"No," I managed to croak.

"So why on earth did you say it was then?"

I burst into tears.

"Lucy? I'm sorry, I didn't mean to upset you."

I shook my head. "It's not you. It's all my fault. I've made a total mess of everything and now it's too late to make things better." I broke into fresh tears.

Millie came and sat next to me, handing me a tissue from a satin box on the bedside table.

"Come on, Lucy. Why don't you tell me about it? I'm sure it's not that bad…"

I paused for a moment. It felt really strange, but I had to tell someone about what had happened and Millie was all I had. I took a deep breath and it all came tumbling out.

"It was the best day of my life," I concluded, after having told her the events of the past few days, "but now Kane will hate me for ever. He must think I'm the most fake girl on the planet and that's the thing he hates most of all — fake girls. And I really think he liked me, you know, just as I am…" I grabbed my hair, "…with this mess and everything…"

Millie laughed. I glared at her.

"I knew you wouldn't understand, Millie. You're always so … so … perfect all the time. Everyone thinks you're so cool. You never put a foot wrong. Think what it's like for me, being your sister. I couldn't be cool if I tried."

Millie smiled at me. "You know, Lucy, this may

surprise you but I think you're pretty cool. That day when you went off to the skatepark and beat the boys. How cool was that? And you looked amazing. No wonder Kane fell for you. Bodey told me one of his friends was there, and according to him those boys thought you were the coolest girl that had ever walked into Sun Peaks. And the prettiest."

I was speechless.

She nodded. "I know, I know. It shocked me as well to realize my hot-headed little sister is growing up and turning heads! And I know you feel that you've made a big mess of things, but you have to let it go. There's nothing you can do. And I know you don't think so now, but you will meet someone else who you like just as much as Kane, maybe even more."

I pretended to agree. But I'd realized as I'd told her the story that I couldn't leave it there. Even if I never saw Kane again it didn't mean that I couldn't put things straight with him. Mum had to have Sarah's phone number somewhere.

There was a knock on the door. Aunt Jo and

Mum popped their heads into the room. "You girls coming for a swim before dinner?" Aunt Jo asked. "There's an infinity pool that they light beautifully at night. It feels like you're swimming right out on the lake."

I looked at Millie and smiled. "We'll be right there!"

Aunt Jo looked pleased. "See, Clemmie, I told you this place would cheer her up."

And I did feel better. A lot better. I had made a decision. As soon as I got to Aunt Jo's house I was going to phone Kane.

14

We had all been reluctant to leave the luxury of the Chateau Hotel the next day. You could get used to a king-size bed and breakfasting on blueberry and maple syrup pancakes and fresh fruit.

We spent the rest of the day visiting the huge waterfall on the Bow River and arrived in the mountain town of Banff that evening. Uncle Hector appeared in front of the large, yellow wooden house to greet us. He stood and stared in amazement at Rambling Rose. "That got you all the way here?" he said in his slow, deliberate manner.

"Hey, don't be rude about her," I replied, "she's been brilliant and hasn't broken down once."

To my frustration he had booked us all dinner in a restaurant in town. Mum kept her bag next to her the whole evening and I couldn't get near it. By the time we got back it was late and time for bed. My call to Kane would have to wait until tomorrow, but that was OK as everyone would be distracted by the barbecue. It would be easy to slip away.

Except it wasn't. From the moment I woke up there were just too many people everywhere.

Millie insisted on helping me get ready; since our talk at Lake Louise we'd been almost "nice" to each other. She blow-dried my hair and put on some mascara and lipgloss. Then she made me put on the new jeans and the white shirt we had bought in Sun Peaks.

"Better," she said. I smiled gratefully, even though I couldn't see the point in making any effort.

As we came downstairs we could hear raised voices. It was Mum and Aunt Jo.

"What's that about?" I whispered.

"Aunt Jo's invited that man Gran wanted Mum to

marry … Howard. He and Uncle Hector are still friends, and now he's divorced he's moved here." Millie grinned. "Mum is distinctly underwhelmed."

That was the trouble with Aunt Jo's surprises. She meant well, but they could be a bit hit and miss.

The garden was already full of people as we stepped out into the bright sunshine.

"Don't tell me!" a man's voice cried out. "You've got to be Clemmie's kids!"

A balding man, with a large stomach straining over his shorts, came towards us. "Is your mother here?"

"Hello, Howard," Mum said in a resigned tone, coming up behind us.

His round face broke into a smile. "Clemmie! Blow me down! You haven't changed a bit."

He immediately launched into a dull monologue revolving around three subjects: one, his divorce; two, how wonderful Mum and he looked for their age; and three, how successful and rich he was.

After five minutes, I realized that Howard was definitely the most boring man I had ever met and by the time he had got on to the subject of his small private plane, "I fly her myself, you know",

I was losing the will to live. I could see Mum and Millie were also desperately looking around for an escape route. Who was going to crack first?

"I've left my bag under the table over there," Mum said suddenly. "I've just got to get something."

Good try, Mum, I thought, but now I could see a brilliant opportunity opening up for me, and it wouldn't just get me away from Howard.

"Don't worry, Mum," I cried cheerfully. "I'll get it."

"I'll come with you, Lucy," Millie said, propelling me away at top speed.

Mum glared at us as we made our escape.

"Wow! Thank goodness she didn't marry him!" Millie giggled. "He would have bored her to death."

We walked towards the table. I could see Mum's bag underneath it but before I could get to it, the air was filled with an ear-splitting scream. "Don!"

Mr Perfect had arrived. Cuba nearly flattened him with a running jump, but when he had recovered and peeled her off I could see that indeed, he was rather perfect — at least on the outside. Fair hair combed smooth, clean white shirt, spotless chinos. If I thought his smile was a bit too smooth as he

said his hellos, I wasn't going to mention it.

"What d'you think?" Millie asked, as Aunt Jo began to herd everyone towards the lunch table.

"Jury's out," I replied.

"Lucy!" Aunt Jo called. "Come and sit here, between Don and Mex."

"Hi." Don gave me an oily smile as I clambered on to the bench beside him. "Am I glad I'm sitting next to you!"

But if he thought for one minute that he was going to be allowed to spend a moment with anyone other than Cuba he had another thing coming. She firmly called his name and he was forced to turn to his other side.

I didn't mind, I had more important things on my mind – like liberating Mum's phone. I bent down and scanned under the table for her bag – there it was, just a couple of metres away. If I reached out with my foot, I could hook it up by the strap. I began to make tentative scooping motions under the table while passing the salad bowl along at the same time. Suddenly, I realized that Don's thigh was pressing firmly against me. Was it my

imagination? I tried to move away but his thigh seemed welded to mine.

I sat, frozen in horror, as without taking his eyes from Cuba, Don's arm dropped down and disappeared under the table – on to my knee. He gave it a squeeze.

"Eeek!" I leaped up.

"What's the matter?" Cuba asked. Don turned to look at me with innocent, pale-blue eyes.

"Yeah, Lucy," he drawled. "What's up?"

"Cramp." I hopped on one foot. "A really horrible pain." I glared at Don. "I'll walk around for a while." I reached for Mum's bag. "Just get this bag. Painkillers," I mumbled.

I looked up the table, but Mum was facing the other way, still trapped by Howard. As I extracted myself from the bench Don had the cheek to wink at me. So much for Mr Perfect.

I walked as quickly as I could for a few steps and then remembered I had cramp and hopped a bit to the kitchen door. Safely inside, I ran upstairs.

"What are you doing?" The mobile clattered to the bedroom floor and Mum picked it up. "I saw you pick up my bag and then Cuba told me that you had cramp. Are you OK?"

How can she see out of the back of her head? I thought. *And thank you, Cuba – who needs a loudspeaker when she's around?*

"Are you OK?" Mum asked again. "You don't need to take painkillers for cramp – you just need to walk around a bit – that'll sort it out."

I nodded. "I'm fine now, thanks."

"Good. Could you pass me my bag? I'm expecting a call from Dad. She paused and frowned. "What were you doing with my phone? You weren't trying to call Maisie…?"

"No, nothing like that…" I babbled, handing her her bag. "I think I left my hoodie at Sarah's, you know the blue one…" It was a desperate excuse. "…And I thought I'd phone Sarah and ask her to post it on to Gran's house. It's my favourite."

"What? Lucy, have you lost your mind? That old hoodie! I'm not going to let you bother Sarah with posting ancient hoodies all over the country.

You've forgotten it and that's that, I'm afraid. It was ready to be chucked out anyway. Posting your hoodie indeed. What are you like?" she muttered as she left the room.

"Anyway," she called back after her, "they've gone away for a few days, up in the mountains, so they're not in phone contact till they get back."

I felt totally deflated. I had been so excited at the thought of hearing Kane's voice again and having the chance to explain everything to him. And now I'd have to wait again.

I wandered back downstairs. Millie was standing in front of the hall mirror, putting on suncream.

"How's the cramp? Coming back to the party?"

"Please, don't make me. At least don't make me sit next to Don again. I don't know how to say this, but Don is NOT Mr Perfect."

"Squeezed your leg under the table, did he?" Millie grinned.

"Yes! How did you guess?"

"Pinched my bum in the kitchen."

"No!"

At that, we both collapsed into giggles.

It felt weird being in Rambling Rose without Aunt Jo, Mex and Cuba. We'd waved them all goodbye that morning, and even though they were all coming to Gran's party, I had to admit I missed them.

I missed Mex peacefully nodding along to his iPod. I missed Aunt Jo's running commentaries on everything and everybody we passed. I even missed Cuba. She didn't mean to be tactless and she certainly didn't deserve a creep like Don. Millie and I had agonized over telling her about what had happened at the party and decided not to.

We couldn't bear to destroy her illusions.

Finally, Mum drove through a pair of large, stone gates and Rambling Rose crunched on to the wide, gravel driveway of a beautiful white house. As we came to a halt in front of it, a tall, elegantly-dressed woman appeared between the large columns of the front porch. Her grey hair was swept up on top of her head in a loose bun, exposing a string of pearls looped around her slender neck. Her sharp, blue eyes took in everything as we clambered out.

"Well, can you believe it?" Gran cried. "You're here at last."

She gave us each a fleeting hug.

"Goodness, just look at these girls of yours, Clemencia, all grown up. How are you, darling? Now I want to hear all about your journey."

She gazed again at Rambling Rose. "So typical of Jo to go for something…" she waved her fingers in the air, "…so very Bohemian. I do hope that you haven't been too uncomfortable."

"It's been great. We've loved living in her," I chirped up loyally.

Gran's eyes swept down and focused on me.

Lucy

Gran's eyes swept down and focused on me. "Well thank goodness for your pioneering spirit, my dear. Like your mother, I suppose."

Mum looked uncomfortable.

"No need to look like that," Gran's voice drifted on, as she ushered us inside the huge house, "we're not going to open old wounds on this visit. I just want to have a lovely party, with all my family and friends, that's all."

Now I was back in the house my early memories of it came flooding back. We entered the hallway with its sweeping wooden staircase and dark paintings.

"We'll have dinner in half an hour. That should give you time to settle in your rooms." She looked us up and down. "And to change."

"She's terrifying, isn't she?" I whispered to Millie, as we followed Gran upstairs to a large blue room with two high brass beds.

"Sure is," Millie replied as she shut the door behind Gran. "But more worryingly, what on earth are we going to change into? We've only got shorts and jeans."

"Well we'll just have to wear the cleanest things

we've got and that will have to do."

So we did, but it was obvious from Gran's face that it didn't "do" at all. And after all the noisy, chaotic meals we'd been used to it was strange to have to concentrate on drinking soup without spilling it and to wonder about which knife to use.

Gran took a sip of her soup and dabbed her mouth with her napkin.

"Now, Clemencia, you must tell me all about your trip. How did you find Jo and Hector? He's made such a success of his insurance business. Jo did marry well. She doesn't have to worry about a thing." Her mouth turned down. "Except losing a few pounds perhaps."

"Jo married Hector for love," Mum said firmly. "And she doesn't do nothing, she's busy too, running her knitwear business." Mum broke her bread roll into pieces. "But thank you for this trip. It's been great to spend time with her and for the children to meet their cousins. And they've seen some spectacular parts of Canada. Haven't you, girls?"

I nodded. "Lake Louise and Bow Falls were beautiful."

Lucy

"Mmmm. Wonderful…" Gran said vaguely, before continuing, "…but what's so nice for Jo is that she doesn't have to work, does she? Which means that she always has plenty of time for her children…"

I caught Millie's eye. Mum wasn't going to like that.

"I've always had time for my children," Mum replied warningly.

Gran put her head on one side. "But you have to work so hard. I do worry about you all—"

"We're fine," I interrupted. "Mum has always been there if we needed her."

"I'm sure she has…" Gran swept on regardless. "…But I can see that times are hard at the moment. I know I said I wouldn't ask but I simply have to. How are things with Nick's business? If only you would let me help you…"

Mum took a deep breath. "Mom, you know Nick wouldn't like that. He's a very proud man."

"Well I know that. But why he won't just take my money I don't know. Still, you did take it this time. And here you are."

"And we're glad and grateful to be here," Mum said firmly. "It is a tough time at the moment but

149

we'll manage. I have faith in him."

Gran rolled her eyes.

"Mom, we're not paupers, you know. We've been fine for years. We're all very happy. It's just that right now we have a big project at a delicate stage, that's all." She shot Gran a warning look. "I really don't want to discuss it any more."

Gran lifted up a hand. "OK, dear. Tell me about Sarah then. I remember her from when you were at school. Now she's married well, hasn't she?"

"And so have I. Nick's a wonderful man." I saw Mum's knuckles tighten and turn white as she gripped her spoon. Gran pretended not to notice.

"If you say so, dear," Gran drawled.

I had had enough.

I banged my spoon down on the table. Gran looked at me, startled.

"Just stop it! Leave Mum alone. She married Dad because she loved him. Like you loved Grandfather. She loves Dad because he's funny and interesting and adventurous and unpredictable. And he has principles and things he believes in.

"Mum told me that Grandfather didn't have a lot

when you married him but you married him anyway. He took risks and chances. According to Mum, you thought he was a wonderful man. Well that's how Mum feels about Dad. So why can't you stop going on about him. Because I find your remarks extremely rude."

There was a deathly hush. Millie and Mum were staring at me open-mouthed. Gran put her hands down on the table, as if to steady herself. She began to shake. I stared at her, horrified. Was she having some sort of fit? She had been mean to Mum, but I didn't want her to keel over right in front of us.

And then I realized that she wasn't having a fit. She was laughing.

"It's not funny," I growled.

She reached out to put a hand on my shoulder. "No, I know, dear. And I'm sorry to laugh. It's very – what was the expression you used – oh yes, 'extremely rude' of me." She looked at Mum.

"Well, what can I say? She's exactly like I was at the same age. And you as well, Clemencia. It's that kind of spirit that has served the Carter family for generations. It got my great grandmother here in

the first place and she built up a ranch from nothing. My word. I swear this girl could run a ranch with one hand tied behind her back." She wiped a tear from her eye.

"Whatever I've said about Nick, Clemencia, I will say this, you've produced girls with guts." She looked at Millie and me thoughtfully, and then smiled. "Perhaps you did marry the right man after all. I know you saw Howard at Jo's barbecue so you know he's divorced now. His ex-wife is as dull as he is. And if I'm honest their children are the feeblest lily-livered creatures you've ever had the misfortune to have drooping around your drawing room."

We were all staring at her in shock.

She scanned each of us in turn, drew herself up, and patted her hands on the table.

"Right, ladies. Tomorrow I've arranged for you to go and spend the day on a real Canadian Ranch."

"Mom!" Mum smiled. "What a great idea."

Gran winked at us. "Thought I'd see what you're really made of…"

It seemed that Mum's family were always full of surprises.

16

Gran woke us up before daybreak. She was already dressed, and looked as if she'd been up for ages.

"Come on, ranch hands start work early and we've got a fair way to go. And pack your swimming things."

We pulled on jeans and T-shirts and hurried downstairs.

"What about breakfast?" Mum asked.

"Breakfast when we arrive," Gran replied. "We need to get going."

We watched the sun rise over the snow-capped

peaks as Gran drove along the road at an alarming speed. By the time she lurched the car down a dusty track, the air was warm and humid. We parked next to several other cars.

A man and woman of around Mum's age came out to greet us.

"Welcome! I'm Rosie, and I'll be looking after you today. Now come on into the ranch house and join everyone else. You must be starving and I've got breakfast on. Will eggs, bacon, biscuits, pancakes and coffee be OK?"

The other guests for the day were three families, including a boy of about ten, two girls and three older boys.

After breakfast, Rosie took us out to saddle up the horses. "I'm going to take you down to a place called Diamond Creek."

Mum laughed and turned to Gran. "Diamond Creek? You used to bring us here to swim when we were young. We're not going to jump off Hangman's Drop, are we? I haven't done that since I was, well … Lucy's age."

"I'm not jumping anywhere today," Gran said

slowly, carefully mounting her horse. I was amazed she was actually going to ride. She must have seen my surprised expression because once she was on she said, "Yes, Lucy. Even old crocks like me can still ride a horse over a mountain." She gathered the reins. "As long as we take it nice and easy."

As neither Millie or I had ridden before, and neither had some of the others, that suited us fine.

The horses strolled through the meadows between the grazing cattle, shaking their heads from time to time to get rid of flies. We had time to talk to the others. The girls were sisters too, older than us, and the boys were sixteen-year-old school friends from Calgary. Their accents reminded me of Kane. I was glad we were doing something interesting today. It would help take my mind off him and make the time pass more quickly until I could call him.

The sun rose high in the sky and I was relieved when we began to descend into shady woods and towards the sound of rushing water.

"Tubes!" one of the boys shouted as we dismounted and tied up the horses. I looked up to

see large, inner-tyre tubes tethered to a small jetty. Perfect for floating down the river. An old hut had been converted into a basic changing room with wetsuits and life jackets.

After a talk from Rosie about what to expect, we were soon swirling around in the water as one by one we were let go. The tubes soon picked up speed as we bounced and eddied along, faster and faster, until suddenly we shot over the edge of a small waterfall, screaming our heads off, and splashed down into a large, calm pool. We dragged our tubes to the riverbank where a man was waiting to load them in his jeep and take us back up again.

I shook the water out of my hair. "That was fantastic!" I shouted.

"It was, wasn't it?" Mum laughed. "We used to do it on old tractor tyres when I came here as a girl."

We all went again before joining Gran and the others for a picnic lunch under the trees.

"So where's this Hangman's Drop?" I asked after we'd eaten.

Mum pointed up the river. "Around the next bend upstream."

"What's that?" the boys asked.

"It's a rock you can jump from," Mum answered. "The river's very deep there."

"Bring it on!" the oldest boy yelled, pulling his unzipped wetsuit back over his shoulders, and grabbing his life jacket. Rosie came over to check we were all of sound mind and body, before letting us head up the path along the riverbank. Even Gran insisted on coming to watch.

"No way!" The sisters stopped in their tracks. "Absolutely no way."

Hangman's Drop was a very, very big rock. It was now clearly in view through the trees, and it was high. A sheer drop into a dark, deep pool.

Even the cocky boys were looking thoughtful now it was in front of them.

Only Mum, Millie, me and two of the boys made the rest of the journey, climbing up the rock and out on to its smooth, flat surface. We could see the others watching below.

The tallest of the boys inched to the edge and looked over. "It's a long way down." He walked back to us and grinned. "You first."

We crept over to the edge. Millie and I stood on either side of Mum and we all peered into the greeny-black water.

"You're not going to do it are you, Mum?" I asked, looking at her anxiously.

"Why not?"

"Well, aren't you a bit..."

"Too old?" She grinned. "I'm not totally decrepit yet, you know. I could still do it."

I leaned over the edge again, my heart beating fast. "Could you?"

"I will if you will," Millie said suddenly. "If we can do this we can do anything."

"All for one and one for all!" I cried.

Mum laughed and looked down again at the expectant faces staring up at us. "Come on then. Let's show them what the pioneering spirit is all about." We all held hands. "On the count of three." Mum took a deep breath. "One, two, three."

"McDonnell girls rule!" I yelled.

And we jumped off.

We emerged from the icy water to a round of applause. When we had scrambled out and

climbed the muddy bank, we all hugged each other with triumphant delight.

Gran looked on happily. Millie turned to her. "Thanks, Gran, you know, for bringing us here. I'm so glad we came. It's been a fantastic experience."

Mum looked at me and pretended to faint, but I could see that what Millie had said had made her really happy.

I was glad. It had been a good day, but in spite of all the distractions, as we rode back to the ranch, my mind kept slipping back to Kane. I knew what I'd said must have really hurt him. What if I called him and he refused to speak to me … what would I do then?

As all this was going through my mind, Gran brought her horse alongside mine. "Right, ladies, now listen up," she barked. "We've had a fun day today but my party is the day after tomorrow. The dress code is black tie. That means looking like James Bond for men and long dresses for you girls." She raised an enquiring eyebrow. "No, I thought not. Good. Looks like we'll have to go shopping." She looked back and frowned at Mum.

"You're surely not going to forbid me from buying gifts for my own daughter and her children on their first visit in seven years?"

Mum shook her head. "Not at all."

Gran cast an approving eye over Millie. "We shall all get our hair done, of course..." Then she looked at me. I saw her taking everything in. "...And take a trip to the beauty parlour. Lucy, I am going to allow you the great privilege of upstaging me. I am going to make you the belle of the ball."

17

Gran was standing in the hall in a dark-green suit, with matching black bag and shoes. She was tapping her foot and looking at her watch.

"Come on, come on. We can't waste a minute." This is my plan for the day. First, dresses. I know where to go for those. Madame Pierre has a wonderful selection and she can do any alterations in no time at all. Which is good, because that is all the time we have. Right, let's go."

"I don't want to go."

Gran closed her eyes and took a deep breath.

"I beg your pardon?"

I shrugged. The truth was, I was scared. Part of me really wanted this makeover – it was a chance to stop being Lucy the scruffy tomboy and grow up. But what if it all went wrong and I ended up looking ridiculous and everyone laughed. And what about Kane ... he'd seemed to like me just as I was...

"I don't really care about the girly thing, Gran ... it's not really me ... I don't mind what I look like."

Gran raised herself to her full height and snapped the clasp on her bag.

"That, my dear, as we used to say on your grandfather's ranch, is the biggest load of horse manure I have ever heard. Get in that car."

At that moment I realized an important truth. I may be tough, but Gran was tougher. I got in the car.

We clung on as she drove us through the streets of Calgary. I could see her glancing at me from time to time in the rear-view mirror.

"What are you thinking about?" she barked suddenly. "You look as if you've got something on your mind."

I blushed. Was she psychic or something? I'd been thinking about Kane, of course, and planning the best time to call. He would be back tomorrow from his trip and I was running through, for the thousandth time, what I wanted to say.

"Well?" Gran went on.

"Nothing."

"Ah, *nothing*," she sighed. "'Nothing' at your age is always a boy. Who is he?"

I looked beseechingly at Millie. "Er..." she said, "I just think that we're all missing Sarah and the boys, Gran. It's going to be a long time before we see them again."

"Hmmm." Gran screwed up her nose. "I see. One of Sarah's sons, is he? Saw them all at the theatre in Calgary last year. Hope it wasn't that ghastly grinning older one? The younger one was rather interesting-looking, though."

I blushed an even deeper red and Mum turned to look at me in quiet surprise.

Gran's eyes flicked up to the mirror again and she nodded before screeching to a halt outside an elegant-looking boutique.

"Mom, this looks awfully expensive…" Mum muttered, as we spilled on to the pavement.

"I should hope so. I haven't seen you all in seven years! And of course," Gran went on, "I know you'll appreciate it. You've inherited my good taste. Unlike your sister. You know she actually knitted me one of her hideous sweaters? Me? With a moose on my chest. Can you believe it?"

Inside the shop there were racks and racks of the most exquisite dresses I'd ever seen. Millie began to flick through the hangers and reverentially mouth the names on each of the labels.

Madame Pierre settled Gran down on a large, white sofa and we began to try them on, emerging out of the changing rooms for her inspection.

"No," she barked.

"No."

"Hideous."

"Mmmm — on to the possibles rack."

"Ghastly. You look like a ball of candyfloss."

"No."

"That one, Millie. That's the one. Madame Pierre?"

And Gran was right. Millie was standing in a long

slip of cream silk with tiny pearls sewn around the neckline. She looked like a Greek goddess.

Then she chose a dark-green taffeta dress for Mum. "You can wear my emerald earrings with it."

And then it was my turn. The rack of chiffon, lace and silk outside my changing room was growing alarmingly.

"No, no, no." Gran gave an exasperated sigh. "Let me look for something. Stay there, Lucy. Don't move."

So I stood in my bra and knickers and waited. Five minutes later a dream of palest-pink silk and net was thrust through the curtain. "Put that on," Gran ordered.

I slipped it over my head. Madame Pierre came in to do up the back. I could see from her expression that she approved.

I stepped out. The dress was tightly fitted to the waist, with thin silk ribbon straps over each shoulder and a matching ribbon that tied around the waist. It then floated out in layers of finest net to mid ankle. It was the sort of dress that made you want to dance around the room or drop into a

deep curtsey like a ballerina. I felt like a princess.

"Lucy!" Mum cried. "It's gorgeous."

Millie nodded. "It truly is. I can't believe it's really you! I'm not sure I've ever seen you in a dress before."

"It will do," Gran said firmly, trying not to look too pleased with herself. "Now we must think accessories… I'm thinking silk pumps, and my pearl studs … and for Millie some strappy heels – possibly gold. Clemencia – black stilettos for you." She smoothed down her skirt and picked up her bag.

"Onwards, girls. Madame Pierre will arrange to deliver the dresses to the house. We have the beautician to get to."

Half an hour later, Gran and I were side by side having manicures. I'd never had a manicure before and it was strange seeing my usually not-too-clean nails being filed and buffed into shape.

"This boy?" she drawled. "Are you missing him terribly?"

"Gran!"

"Are you?"

"Yes."

"And is he missing you?"

"No. I think he must hate me."

"Hate you! Oh dear. That's not good. Why?"

"I made a bit of a mess of things when I was there; there was a misunderstanding. I hurt his feelings."

Gran gave me a look that said she wasn't going to be fobbed off with any waffle. "I need you to start at the beginning and tell me absolutely everything. I am unshockable."

So I did.

After I had finished she sat quietly thinking for a while before saying, "And what do you intend to do about the situation, because you don't strike me as the kind of girl who wouldn't be thinking of doing something."

"I'm going to call him," I blurted out. "Tomorrow night. I'm going to get Sarah's number and explain everything."

"During my party?"

I bit my lip. Had I blown it?

"I don't know... I hadn't really thought about—"

"Well, if you are going to sneak off, use the landline in the study. It's very private. The rest of the house will be full of people. No one will be going in there. Now, this kind lady is going to cover my face with mud from the bottom of the Dead Sea. So I am going to relax and enjoy some peace."

I turned to look at her. Gran's face was now being painted with a black mask and her eyes were firmly closed.

"Thanks, Gran."

She waved a hand in regal dismissal.

I didn't recognize myself.

There was a girl staring out at me from the mirror, but it couldn't be me.

"Just beautiful." Mum clasped her hands together. She looked like she was going to cry.

"Did I look so bad before?" I pulled a face.

"Of course not. It's just that you look so … so … grown up."

It was the day of the party and Jerome, Gran's hairdresser, had just left.

"Your hair looks amazing," said Millie. Jerome

had cut long layers into the front and blow-dried it as sleek and straight as Millie's.

"You look great, too…"

"We all look sensational!" Gran swanned in wearing a slim-fitting, coffee-coloured silk dress. A loop of her trademark pearls hung down the front, tied with a knot halfway down. She looked at my reflection in the mirror. "But I have to say, Lucy, you will be the belle of the ball."

I looked again at the girl in the mirror. I looked at the way the skirt of her dress spread out so beautifully around her as she sat on the chair. I looked at her face. Her large, brown eyes with just a touch of mascara, a brush of blusher on her cheeks and a hint of lipstick. That was all Gran said was needed and she had been right. I loved the way this girl looked. I just couldn't quite believe that it was me…

"No one is going to call you 'Boy' any more, that's for sure," Millie said approvingly.

And that was the best thing of all. No one was laughing or saying I looked ridiculous. My worst fears hadn't come true.

Lucy

And tonight I would get to talk to Kane, at last, and I could explain everything. It wouldn't make up for losing that precious last morning, but at least I would hear his voice again.

Gran's house was full of activity as florists and caterers put the last-minute touches to everything. In all the hustle and bustle it was easy to slip into Mum's room and find Sarah's number on her phone. I wrote it down and stuffed it into one of my pumps. As I went downstairs the doorbell started ringing, and suddenly I was trapped on the bottom step by Gran and Mum, being introduced to millions of people I didn't know. Howard's ex-wife arrived with their drippy children trailing behind her. Gran gave me a meaningful "See what I mean?" look. Then Aunt Jo spilled into the hall with her family. They all stood and gawped at me.

"Speechless, Jo?" Gran smiled, taking in Jo's flowing floral kaftan. "So rare for our family."

"You look amazing!" Cuba gasped.

"So do you," I replied. I saw Gran's eyes flick over Cuba's lime-green and orange prom dress and raise an eyebrow at me. Gran was a terrible

character sometimes.

"Looking good, cousin." I stared at Mex. Were my ears deceiving me?

"Thanks, Mex!" I gasped.

I had to make my escape. Muttering something about needing to speak to someone, I slipped out of the hall, down the corridor and into the study. In the middle of the room was a mahogany desk with a large, leather swivel chair in front of it. Sitting on the desktop was the phone. I sank down into the chair and pulled off my shoe. My heart was pounding. I took some deep breaths, picked up the phone and dialled the number. It rang and rang. "Please be in, please be in..." I whispered, and then, just as I was about to give up I heard a click.

"Hi. This had better be good. I'm in the middle of watching a movie here."

"Bodey?"

"Yeah. Who's this?"

"Lucy."

"Lucy? Well hi, Lucy. What can I do for you?"

I was finding it hard to speak. "I, er ... was wondering if Kane was around?"

Lucy

"Kane? Nope, sorry. You missed him. He's just gone out. Skatepark probably."

My spirits sank. No prizes for guessing who might be at the skatepark.

"Want me to take a message?" Bodey sounded puzzled. "Or I can give you his mobile number? Though he doesn't usually answer…"

I scrabbled for a pen. "Yes please. That'd be great."

I scrawled the number down. "Thanks, Bodey. Bye."

I pressed the phone to the front of my dress. I could feel my heart beating against it. I had to act quickly before I lost my nerve completely. I carefully dialled the new number. It rang twice.

"Hello?"

I gripped the phone.

"Hello. Kane?"

"Lucy?"

I was suddenly paralyzed with embarrassment at hearing his voice again. What was I doing? But I had rehearsed this conversation in my head a million times, and I wasn't going to back out now.

I took a deep breath.

"Kane, I'm phoning you to say sorry, you know, about how I behaved and the things I said that last morning, I know you must have heard..."

"You're entitled to your opinion." He sounded frosty.

"But it wasn't my opinion, Kane. I was hurt and angry and there was this huge Tara mix-up."

"What Tara mix-up? What does she have do with anything?"

"I thought that you were going on a date with her, the day we left."

"Did you? And why would you think that?"

"Because I overheard Bodey talking to her brother. He said you were going to meet her."

"Well, maybe if you had just asked me about it first instead of assuming the worst about me, you may have saved us both a tough morning."

"I'm really sorry." I gathered up my courage. "What I said about that day on the lake?"

"Oh yes, what was that? I remember now, 'the most dull and boring day of your life'."

"No! No. I know that's what I said, but I didn't

mean it, it wasn't like that at all."

"Oh really? What kind of a day was it then?"

"It was the best kind."

There was a pause.

"Even though it wasn't with your dream date — my big brother?"

"I didn't mean that either."

"Seems to me you said and did a lot of things you didn't mean."

"I know! I know! And if I wasn't so hot-headed and had thought a bit first, none of this would have happened."

"True."

"I can only say I'm very sorry. I messed up. I guess I'm never going to be one of those girls who can be cool about things."

"Good."

"Pardon?"

"I like that."

"Like what?"

"I like the fact you get all mad about things. That you can never, ever hide what you're feeling."

"Even though I hurt you?"

"No. I didn't like that one bit. My advice is still get mad, but make sure you've got your facts right first. But I'm talking to you now so let's just leave it."

"Can you? Really?"

"Sure. I forgave you when you bit my arm the last time I saw you. I can forgive you this time, too."

"Hey, I only bit your arm because you punched me first."

"Mmmm, that's true but you were a pain then as well. Here's an idea. Let's try really hard to get it right next time we meet, OK?"

Next time we meet? My heart sank. "Do you think it will be another seven years before we see each other?"

"I don't think so."

"How can you know?"

"I just have a feeling I'll see you sooner than that."

"But why?"

"Because I've been standing at the door for five minutes and I can see you now."

I gasped and span the chair around. A circle of fine net floated around with me. And there he was ... exactly like the last time I had seen him, except

this time he was wearing a dinner suit and he was staring as if he couldn't believe his eyes.

"Lucy! You look ... you look..."

"Like a doll?" I winced.

"No! Are you kidding? You look well ... totally amazing. But you always looked amazing, even soaking wet and mad in a canoe."

"You said I looked like an irritated seal."

"But you were the prettiest irritated seal I'd ever seen," he laughed.

I wanted to leap up and fling my arms around him, but instead I found myself glued to my seat. I stammered, "B-but what are you doing here?"

He switched his phone off and I put mine back on the desk. "We got back from our trip a day early to find a message from your grandmother suddenly and urgently needing my mom to come to her party. Your gran said to bring me. Wow. I can't stop staring at you."

I couldn't help smiling.

"And you came? After what I said?"

"We-ell, I wasn't too keen at first, to be honest. Didn't think you wanted to see me. But your sister

came on the phone and … explained things to me a little. Do these doors open on to the garden?"

He pushed the French windows apart and we could hear the music from the party.

"Want to dance? I feel like we're kind of dressed for it, except I can't stand this dumb bow tie any more." He tore it off and undid the neck button on his shirt. "Look at what I've had to wear to get to see you again," he complained. "If the guys at Sun Peaks could see me now…" He raised an eyebrow at me and reached for my hand. I stepped out into the lantern-lit garden as if I was walking on air. "Hey, Cinderella, are you missing a shoe…?"

Much later, after dancing and talking the night away, we collapsed on a bench under the trees.

"Did Bodey know you were here?"

"Of course he did."

"Well, he's not all bad then, is he? He's certainly a good actor."

Kane leaned back and contemplated the stars. "It's kind of a perfect night, isn't it?"

I nodded.

"There's only one thing troubling me."

I turned towards him, frowning. "What's that?"

"Been on my mind for a while now."

"What?"

"It's that punch I gave you all those years ago."

"What about it?"

"It was quite a cut, wasn't it? I've always felt bad about it. Guilty, you know. Guilty that I might have caused some long-term injury." He looked down at my face.

"In fact," he continued as his hand reached to touch my cheek, "I think I'd better check for possible scarring, just to put my mind at rest. Is that OK?"

"I think it's the only decent thing to do," I replied solemnly.

He traced his finger around the edge of my mouth, frowning like a doctor executing a serious examination. He was so close I could feel his breath. "What's the diagnosis?" I asked.

"Perfect." He smiled and kissed me.

19

Kane was standing in front of me in the study, back in his baggy jeans and faded shirt. It was four days since Gran's party. I knew we were both listening for the sound of tyres on the driveway. The airport taxi was due in five minutes.

"Guess it really is goodbye now," he said gravely, pushing a strand of hair off my face. "But we had four days we thought we'd never have, didn't we?"

I nodded. He knew I was trying not to cry.

"I hope they haven't been too dull and boring?" He managed a smile.

I looked up into his dark-blue eyes. When would I see them again?

"They were the best days…" I bit my lip.

He nodded. "Thank goodness my mom didn't mind staying for a few extra days, too."

I took a nervous breath. "Mum will miss her a lot." I paused. "Will you miss anyone?"

He frowned. "Do you even have to ask?"

Then he smiled again.

"If you really want to know, I shall miss that irritating girl with the messy hair who first arrived at Sun Peaks; I shall miss the skater girl who thrashed Paul on the half-pipe; I shall miss the angry, wet, sulking girl in the canoe; I shall miss that sophisticated girl who spun round to face me in that chair…"

"Which one will you miss the most?"

"Lucy!" Kane gave an exasperated sigh. "I can't miss one of them, because they are all you. You know, beautiful, clever, funny; the girl I can talk to about anything."

I wanted to hug those words and keep them close to me for ever.

"But I do look different now." I looked down at my new clothes.

He took my hands and drew back. "The old tomboy-you hasn't gone away. It's still part of you and I love that!"

He pulled me towards him and kissed me.

"Lucy! Taxi's here!" Mum's voice broke the spell.

We drew apart. Kane stared at me as if he wanted to remember every single detail.

"I guess this is it."

"I guess it has to be."

"Lucy! Where are you?" Mum yelled again.

"Come on then," Kane said, taking my hand, "it's time to go."

It was chaos on the driveway. Sarah immediately called Kane over to help her with her bags. Aunt Jo, Mex and Cuba were rushing around saying goodbyes to everyone. Uncle Hector was already sitting up in the driving seat in Rambling Rose. He was driving her back to Banff, back to her owners. He switched on the engine and we heard her roar and splutter into life for the last time. She began to crunch towards the gates. Millie and I

found ourselves running after her with our hands on her sides shouting, "Goodbye, goodbye!" at the tops of our voices. And then she was gone in a cloud of exhaust smoke.

We stood at the gate and watched her disappear. I looked at Millie.

"What on earth did we do that for?"

Millie burst out laughing. "I don't know!"

"Because Rambling Rose has tremendous karma, that's why." Aunt Jo had crunched up to Millie and me. She was holding two large parcels in her arms.

"Look at the two of you! You girls seem to be getting on a whole lot better now than when you first arrived. Am I right?"

We looked at each other. Millie grinned at me.

"You're right, Aunt Jo. I do think that we might be."

"I told you this trip would be good for your inner spirit. The great Canadian outdoors. It's being with nature, you see. It feeds the soul."

We all looked over at Cuba, who was talking on her mobile.

Aunt Jo nodded. "Mmmm, poor child. Cuba's had some bad news while we've been here. Don't

know if she mentioned it?"

Mentioned it? Her wails had been heard all over Gran's house. And it's a big house. One of her friends had decided to let Cuba in on the truth about Don. He had been seen dating another girl.

Aunt Jo looked over at her daughter again and shook her head. "I do hope this won't have a long-term effect on Cuba. She has such a sensitive nature."

At that point Cuba came bounding up, grinning from ear to ear.

"Good news?" Millie asked.

"Definitely. Sarah-Louise has dumped Don."

"You're not going to go out with him again are you?" I gasped. "Because—"

"Are you kidding? I'm going out with Joe Black now. That was him on the phone. Honestly, Lucy, he is totally the most perfect boy you've ever met..."

"I thought Don—" Millie frowned.

"Please. That's just *so* over..."

Aunt Jo put her head on one side and beamed fondly. "She has such strength of spirit ... but hey, look at me with these parcels." She thrust them at

Lucy

us. "For you. A gift from me."

Millie caught my eye. We slowly unwrapped them to reveal two enormous chunky sweaters. We held them up to our chests. Millie's had a moose on it, and mine a black bear.

I couldn't help smiling. "They're great, Aunt Jo. Really, really great. Thanks." We both gave her a huge hug.

"Jo, you shouldn't have." Mum came up with Gran, Sarah and Kane.

"Don't you worry, Clemmie. No need for you to be jealous. I've got one for you, too. I'll just get it."

Gran gave Mum a wicked smile.

"You are a terrible, terrible woman!" Mum frowned at her, trying not to laugh. "But thank you for a wonderful visit and for, well … everything."

Gran hugged her tight. "Good luck, my dear. Don't leave it another seven years."

And then everyone was hugging everyone and I said, "Thank you, thank you," a million times to Gran, and Mex came up to Millie and me and said, "Great vacation cousins, the best." And Cuba began howling, saying she'd miss us all too much.

I'd already got into the taxi when she suddenly threw herself in front of it and shrieked that Kane and I should have a keepsake, like half a locket, that we could put together when we next saw each other. She started running frantically around the driveway searching for something suitable.

Kane raised his eyebrows at me through the taxi window, and we turned to watch her pick up a stone. She placed it on the porch, and reached for a large rock, which she dropped from a height on to the stone. She tenderly gathered up the tiny pieces and then she walked over and dribbled a small handful of crushed rubble into my hand, and poured the rest into Kane's.

"It's the best I could do," she sighed.

"Thanks, Cuba," we said together.

And then the taxi pulled away and they were gone.

"Oh my goodness. What have you done with Lucy while you were away?"

Dad was swinging me around at the airport. "I don't recognize you."

"It's only my hair that's a bit different," I protested.

"And your clothes," Mum added.

"And a smidgen of make-up," Millie concluded, extracting her limbs from around Finn, who had turned up at the airport carrying a bunch of limp red roses.

"And I don't remember there being quite so

many suitcases when you left."

Dad and Finn were loading them on to a trolley.

There was an awkward silence.

"You know what my mother's like." Mum shrugged. "And the girls did need some new stuff. I couldn't stop her from spoiling her grandchildren…"

"Still hates me, does she?" He grinned.

"No, not so much this time. In fact she's rather pro you now," Mum replied. "We kind of turned a corner. Thanks to Lucy, mainly…"

Dad looked surprised. "Really? That should be an interesting story. Actually, I've got an interesting story of my own for you."

"I knew something was up when you wouldn't answer my calls." Mum frowned anxiously. "What's been going on?"

"You remember that councillor who was blocking my plans? Graham? Well it turns out he had taken a huge bribe from Grandecourts — that build-'em-cheap outfit that were going to get the contract. He's been arrested. There's a new guy taken over. Who knows? It could be good for us."

"That's great, Nick," Mum said, putting her arm through his. "But we'll be fine whatever happens. She looked round at all of us. "We've got everything we need."

In the back of the car, Millie snuggled happily under Finn's arm. I felt a pang of jealousy; Kane seemed so far away. I was glad Maisie and Lucas were coming over. I wondered what they'd make of the new me? Would Lucas laugh?

He didn't. In fact he didn't make any sound at all for some time. Maisie jumped up and down the moment she saw me. "Wow! You look amazing! I can't believe it. Everyone at school is just going to DIE when they see you. Doesn't she look incredible, Lucas?"

He nodded dumbly.

Maisie frowned. "Are you OK?"

He shook himself. "What? Yeah, sure. You just look so … so…"

"Beautiful is the word you're looking for, I believe," said Maisie, grinning.

I couldn't believe it. Was Lucas actually blushing? I had to tell him the skatepark story to

settle him down. It was great to see him again but I was glad when he had to leave. I was desperate to tell Maisie about Kane.

"Bye, Lucas." I waved after him.

"Bye ... B-b-b..." There was an awkward pause. "Lucy." He grinned at me. I smiled back.

Maisie was brilliant. She listened as I recounted every detail of my holiday and every moment I had spent with Kane.

"At least you can email and message and stuff," she said sympathetically when I'd finished. "And you will see him again one day."

"But it could be years! I don't think I can bear it."

"Lucy, I promise you, you're going to meet loads and loads of boys."

"Did you meet anyone?" I asked. "In Scotland?"
She nodded.

"Well come on!" I yelled. "Tell me all, was he dreamily gorgeous?"

She nodded. "He was. He was totally dreamily gorgeous and I went absolutely crazy for him and his Scottish accent. We had romantic meetings on the beach every day."

"So are you going to see him again?"

She shook her head sadly. "Er … no. We had one magical week of bliss together and then I'm afraid a big shadow fell over our relationship and it was all over."

"Oh dear, what was it?"

"His girlfriend, Hettie. And when I say a big shadow, I mean big." Maisie raised her eyes to the ceiling and wailed, "When am I going to meet a boy who doesn't lie to me, and more importantly, doesn't have a scary girlfriend?"

"You will, Maisie, honestly," I said. "There are lovely, gorgeous, honest boys out there and you'll find one soon."

"And so will you."

I thought about Kane, and that day on the lake, and the way he was so intense about everything one minute and how he could make you laugh out loud the next. "Not like that one," I sighed. "I'll never meet another boy like him."

"Well, at least you can write brilliant letters to him. You are the queen of the romantic letter, after all. You've written loads for other people, now you

can write them from yourself, can't you? You won't have to pretend to be anyone else."

Maisie was right. I thought of all the words I'd written to people I didn't care about. Now I had someone of my own to write to, someone I cared about a lot.

When Maisie had gone I switched on my computer. I smiled when I thought about the day when Miss Marshall caught me writing that letter to Brad. I had changed a lot since then. There were going to be no glass coaches or pink doves in what I was going to say today. Just great memories of a special summer and everything it had meant to me.

I tapped the keyboard. "Dear Kane…"